SECOND FLAME

PHOENA'S QUEST
BOOK 2

Chrissy Garwood/Chrisolite Books
Sorell, Tasmania, Australia, 7172
www.chrissygarwood.com

Cover Design: Donita Bundy

Second Flame: Phoena's Quest Book 2/ Chrissy Garwood. —1st ed.

ISBN: 978-0-6489651-4-5 (paperback)
978-0-6489651-5-2 (eBook)

SECOND FLAME

PHOENA'S QUEST
BOOK 2

CHRISSY GARWOOD

CHRISOLITE BOOKS

Sorell, Tasmania, Australia

Dedicated to my Nephew Marcus.

CONTENTS

PRONUNCIATION GUIDE

Phoena – fee-nah

Nessandra – ness-an-drah

Yiana – yee-ah-nah

Ivandelle – eye-van-dell

Andressan – ann-dress-ann

Oramis – o-ram-is (short o as in hop)

Baraapa – bar-ah-pah

Karilion – kar-ill-yon

CHAPTER 1:
AN UNLIKELY CHAMPION

"What *are* you *wearing?*"

Phoena leapt to her feet, abandoning the chair outside the headmistress's office. The question came from a short girl hidden beneath a bright pink hat, top-heavy with silk flowers and ribbons. Phoena's mouth twitched. *You ask me that question?*

She bobbed down to look under the brim and hesitated. Instead of a child, she was face to face with a shapely young woman wearing a pink outfit that matched the hat. The stranger took a step back and grinned up at her.

Phoena smoothed her hands over her brown dress. "What's wrong with what I'm wearing?"

"It looks as if your grandmother chose it for you!"

How much of the truth should Phoena reveal? She straightened, her heart dancing – having someone to belong to was still new. "My godfather did the choosing," she said, forcing the laughter from her voice. "And my godmother said it was 'perfectly serviceable' for this occasion. To refuse to wear it would be *ungrateful.*"

The pink hat bobbed as the wearer laughed and clapped her hands. "You are a funny thing. But you have good taste in paintings." She indicated the seascape on the wall opposite Phoena's chair. "I sneak through here all the time. If you stand in just the right spot, the ship rocks on the waves."

Phoena forced a smile as her chest became a prison for her bolting heart. How magically sensitive was this stranger?

Remember to breathe! She clasped her tingling hands behind her back.

As they stood side by side, Phoena silently prayed what her godmother called an "arrow prayer":

> Aemeithriel, Creator and Sustainer, your servant begs for wisdom and discernment.

Her godmother's warning rang in her mind as they faced the painting in the gilded frame. Not everyone would understand her faith or appreciate Phoena's gifts.

The energy emanating from the artwork was intense. The salt-laden breeze ruffled the ribbons on the pink hat, but her companion seemed not to notice. Neither did she remark about the screeching seabirds as they dived in and out of the waves.

By the time the stranger turned from the painting with a sigh, Phoena knew how to proceed. She gestured towards the pink outfit. "Is that what I should be wearing?"

The curvaceous young woman giggled. "Only if you're a trendsetter." Her full skirts lifted as she twirled, revealing layers of frilly petticoats. Her lacy pantaloons disappeared into high-heeled pink boots. "The Princess Royal wore a blue outfit like this one last week. We share the same dressmaker." She placed her hands on her hips and struck a pose. Pinched tight at the waist, the dress featured a bodice with a low, scooped neckline. "In a week or two, all the fashionable ladies will be copying this style."

Shaking her head, Phoena said, "I think this dress suits me better."

The other woman grinned. "I like a girl who knows her mind. Luckily I found you before you met anyone from the Inner Circle. They love tormenting new girls. Come with me, and I'll introduce you to my friend, Yiana." She grabbed Phoena's arm to lead her away.

The "new girl" planted her feet firmly on the polished wooden floor. "I'm not going anywhere until Lady Cecily finishes her interview with the headmistress."

This statement unleashed a flood of words. "I knew it was you! Your guardian is Lady Cecily de Montnoir, recently returned to Sumnarscote." The stranger glanced eagerly towards the closed door. Her smile was contagious. "You're the mysterious protégé."

"That's me," Phoena said, dropping into a small curtsey. "Miss Phoena Ashton, at your service. And you are?"

"Oh, sorry. I forgot you're not from around here." The words flowed like a river escaping through a narrow ravine. "I'm Lady Nessandra Cascade, but you can call me Nessie. Everyone does. And I'm the first to meet you! What luck! We're in *all* the same classes so you can sit with me. I was going to ask you anyway."

Phoena nodded. She imagined herself as a painted ship carried along by the torrent of Nessie's enthusiasm. A most unexpected welcome!

"My previous study companion left last semester," Nessie continued. "She's preparing for her wedding. No further education required. That happens so regularly they bunch the older girls together as seniors. We've been told ALL about you. At almost seventeen, you're practically an old maid. I'm glad you've come. You've saved me from having to fraternise with my cousin Meredith."

Would "cousin Meredith" be disappointed – or relieved?

"It's probably a good thing that you're *only* a day student," Nessie said.

Aha! The first hint of trouble brewing. Would Nessie abandon her when the other disadvantages came to light?

Nessie continued her impassioned monologue. "But I shall be your champion—"

Champion! Phoena dropped back into the chair.

"Hey, don't worry." Nessie patted Phoena on the shoulder and lowered her voice. "With me on your side, everything will be fine. The other girls may see you as a threat, but your social connections already elevate you above them. I can't wait until they *see* you – that old-fashioned dress only enhances your charm. Every eligible nobleman in the kingdom will fall at your feet and offer you his heart."

Phoena chewed her lip. "I'm not here to win hearts."

"Aha! I knew it! There's more to your story. We've speculated about your late enrolment – the rest of us have been here since nursery school." She patted Phoena's arm. "Your secret's safe with me. I know how to keep unwelcome suitors away. The other girls think I'm strange – unmarried at nineteen! If a girl's not betrothed by the time she's sixteen..." Her voice dropped to a whisper. "It's not that I haven't had offers, but I don't like to kiss and tell. I'm in no hurry. I want to have at least one adventure before I settle down."

The office door opened. Lady Cecily emerged, with the headmistress close behind her. The waiting room atmosphere chilled, matching the snowless winter's day outside. Both adults frowned when they saw Nessie, who fell silent as she dipped into a quick curtsey.

Phoena's godmother was handsome, tall and broad-shouldered with an ample bosom. Today, she wore a blue ensemble: a tailored jacket and a straight, floor-length skirt.

The only relief from the severity were pearl buttons and a white shirt collar. Her braided hair coiled about her head beneath a small blue and white hat.

For many years, Cecily had disguised herself as the daunting Matron at an all-male school, the exclusive *Westernbrooke Academy for Young Noblemen*. There, she had used her height to enhance her carefully cultivated persona. The students had been cocky and self-important, but all of them had meekly obeyed her. Even the esteemed Masters had quaked when she addressed them.

There were unasked questions in Cecily's eyes as Phoena's godmother silently reiterated the need for discretion. Pencil-thin Viola Hammersley had already been headmistress when Cecily had been a student decades earlier. Phoena knew that the stern headmistress would be difficult to please.

Phoena's cheeks coloured as her fingers behind her back played with the grey bangle on her wrist. The ornament was one of three keepsakes from her old life. Lord Karilion's bangle was a family heirloom forged from a fallen star. Hidden beneath her high-buttoned bodice, she wore the medallion Viscount Baraapa had crafted. Pinned to her underdress was Lord Oramis' glittering dragon brooch.

Each of her three self-declared champions had been dynamically drawn to Phoena. Having been her companions when her powers were awakening, they were never far from her thoughts. These noblemen believed she was the fulfilment of an ancient prophecy.

According to the prophecy, Phoena would attract four champions. Karilion, Baraapa and Oramis had speculated about the identity of the missing candidate. Cecily insisted that the fourth champion would reveal themselves at the "right time".

Nessie squeezed Phoena's arm, bringing her back to reality with a jolt.

Mrs Hammersley addressed Phoena's companion. "Lady Nessandra Cascade, I've long ceased to be surprised to find you loitering here. This time, your presence might prove useful. Show Miss Ashton to her rooms on the third floor. I expect to see you both in the dining room in half an hour."

Without waiting to see if they obeyed her command, the headmistress turned to Cecily. "I can assure you that there is no reason to be concerned, Lady de Montnoir. The young ladies here at Quenthlaretta College will make Miss Ashton welcome..."

CHAPTER 2:
HIGHER EXPECTATIONS

Phoena hurried after Nessie, feeling like a dinghy bobbing in the wake of a mighty yacht. Her guide tackled three flights of stairs with great urgency. The girls they encountered jumped aside, shouting remarks which revealed Nessie's renown.

"Hey, watch where– Oh, it's YOU!"

"Look out! Nessie's coming!"

"Why do I need rooms?" Phoena asked Nessie. "I'm a day student."

"You still need somewhere to change your outfits during the day," Nessie explained, "and a drawing room to fulfil your social obligations. The alliances you forge here are more important than any lessons in algebra and history."

They rushed along a wide hallway. Phoena was breathless by the time they stopped at the final door. Nessie pointed to the brass nameplate: "Miss Ashton."

Nessie smiled and stepped aside. Phoena paused, her fingers tracing the engraved letters. She was unused to the formal designation. Until recently, she had held no social status – an indentured servant at the *Westernbrooke Academy* – an orphaned girl without a family name.

Gripping the door handle, Phoena pushed into the suite.

She stopped in the middle of a generous reception room decorated in soft pastel tones. The room was uncomfortably cold – all the windows were open.

A clatter brought her attention to an ornate fireplace, and a maid struggling to light the fire. Phoena felt a stab of anguish – the chambermaid's expression revealed a mixture of embarrassment and fear. The servant wore a white apron over a plain ankle-length dress, not dissimilar to Phoena's old uniform.

Memories from fourteen years of servitude pummelled Phoena. Her knees buckled as she fought the weakness. It had been easier to deal with her emotions before her mythical powers revealed themselves. Her body was still recovering from the injuries sustained during that awakening... She had no wish to repeat the adventure – being evacuated to an underground cave had proven unbelievably dangerous.

Tearing her attention from the servant, Phoena feigned interest in the other furnishings.

"Daisy, leave us," Nessie said. "Come back and fix the fire later."

The maid curtsied and hastily retreated. When the door closed, Nessie pulled off her hat and sent it whizzing across the room. A floral arrangement fell over, pouring water onto the table. Phoena retrieved the hat, rescued the flowers and righted the upturned vase. She glanced over her shoulder and frowned – Nessie hadn't noticed the mess she had made. Instead, that reckless woman had thrown herself onto a sofa, and her boots rested on the padded seat.

While Nessie was looking towards the smoking fire, Phoena used her power to redirect the water back to the vase. But her temper was rising, driven by her undisciplined power. Phoena strode to the fire and seized the poker. With a few deft twitches of her hand, the black coals beneath the smoking timber whooshed into flame.

"Hey!" Nessie exclaimed. "Did you use a fire-lighting spell?"

Phoena hid her hands in the folds of her skirt. "I don't need magic to light a fire – I've had a lot of practice." She blushed at the memory of a dragon who had admired her fire-lighting skills. She steadied her breathing. Oramis, the shapeshifting dragon-lord, would have had a better answer.

The other girl stared at Phoena in wonder. "Lucky you! Fancy being allowed to play with fire! I've always wanted to learn how to light one, but Father forbade the servants from teaching me. He said he didn't want me burning the house down."

Phoena couldn't remember a time when she wasn't tending a blaze. From the age of three, she had kept the impressive *Westernbrooke Academy* kitchen fires burning. A few beatings had taught her not to let the coals burn too low. She had expected to end her days in the overheated kitchens. But, five years ago, an unprecedented promotion to housemaid had brought her release. Only later did she discover that her godmother was responsible.

After adding wood to the fire, Phoena handed the poker to Nessie.

The young woman tentatively prodded the coals. One of the logs shifted, and sparks exploded into the room. "Oh!" Nessie screamed, dropping the poker and leaping away. "I'll leave fire lighting to the maids."

How would Nessie respond if she knew the truth? That the new student had been a servant not so long ago. Phoena bit her tongue, reminded that freedom brought different challenges.

The talkative nineteen-year-old explored the suite, opening doors. "You're so *lucky* to have all this space to yourself."

Phoena flinched. That phrase again! Someone from her servant life had called her "lucky". At the time, she hadn't agreed. But her guardians insisted everything she had endured was preparation for her destiny.

"Are you sure I don't have to share this with someone?" Phoena asked.

"There was only one name on the door." Nessie laughed, bouncing on the massive bed in the master bedroom. The older teenager ran to a second bedroom that was also well furnished. A smaller door led to a bedroom set aside for a personal maid. "Look, you have a private washroom and an impressive dressing room."

Two large trunks rested on the carpet in the dressing room. Phoena's name was on the tags. Nessie lifted a lid and voiced her approval. "Oh, good!" She rifled through the dresses inside. "You won't have to wear that brown dress all day! After lunch, I'll help you decide what to wear for your first lessons."

"I have to change dresses?"

"Of course." Nessie stared at Phoena. "Where have you been hiding? No one in civilised society would wear the same outfit all day. You have to change before dinner, too."

The colour drained from Phoena's face. What else didn't she know about "civilised society"? To start this new life, only days before her seventeenth birthday–

Nessie rushed over. "You've gone so pale! Shall I summon a maid?"

"No!" Phoena said. "I'll be fine. Too much excitement..."

She pushed back the familiar darkness, devoting her energy towards tending the fire.

Nessie's voice came from near the window. "You have a view of the river."

"Is your room on this floor?" Phoena asked.

"Halfway along this hallway, on the opposite side. My windows look towards my family estate. I can even see the King's Citadel in the distance." Nessie turned back to Phoena. "This semester, I'm sharing with Meredith, and neither of us is happy with that – *she's* one of the Inner Circle."

"Meredith is your cousin–"

"Oh, don't worry about Meredith," Nessie said, launching into another lengthy speech. "She has plenty of friends. We don't have anything in common. Mother was hoping Meredith would be a good influence on me – I'm the wayward one who refuses to conform. Mother's worried that I'll end up a social outcast. But I keep reminding her that I'm one of the Princess Royal's favourites, so I can't go wrong. That only makes my mother worry even more.

"Princess Ivandelle is forty-four, and she's unmarried. Of course, the Princess's situation is complicated. She's been taking care of her brother, the King. If the Princess had been born first, she would have married early to secure her line of succession. Then her brother could have quietly withdrawn from society.

"Anyway, my mother will be appeased when she learns who your godmother is."

"Why would knowing who my godmother is 'appease' your mother?"

"You don't know? I don't suppose Lady de Montnoir likes to talk about her past," Nessie said. "She was a student here, a contemporary of the Princess Royal. Your godmother was a great favourite at Court. Mother said everyone expected Lady Cecily to marry the King, but that was *before* his accident.

"He wasn't supposed to survive, and he ordered her to marry someone else. She chose an older nobleman who belonged to some secret organisation. They went adventuring to distant lands. No one knows when her husband died, but he must have left her well provided. Everyone admires a wealthy widow who can manage her finances."

"And what are they saying about me?" Phoena asked.

"At first, people thought you were her daughter, but there's no family resemblance. You're nothing like anyone in her family or the de Montnoirs. They say that your skin is too fair, and none of them has blue eyes. There are lots of other theories. If Lady de Montnoir is *really* your godmother, then, *of course,* you must be the child of some foreign nobility. Why else would a woman of her social standing take on a protégé?

"Then there's the most outrageous suggestion of all." Nessie chortled. "She picked you up from an orphanage so she wouldn't have to return alone. If she wants to maintain the mystery, that's her business. Perhaps we should dye your dark hair blonde? No? Only trying to help. It can't have been easy for her to return after such a long absence."

"I've been so busy thinking about how my life has changed," Phoena said, "I haven't considered what it must be like for Cecily."

"She obviously cares for you a great deal, sparing no expense to make you comfortable here." Nessie gazed around the room. "This suite has been empty for years. The Princess Royal was the last resident – not even my family can afford the fees."

Someone knocked at the door. Before Phoena could react, Nessie opened it. A footman stood in the hallway.

"The Headmistress has summoned you, Lady Cascade," he said. "Everyone is waiting for you and Miss Ashton to join them in the dining room for luncheon."

"Thank you," Nessie said. "We'll be along directly." She closed the door again. "Where did I put my hat? I can't make a grand entrance without it. Half the fun of a new outfit is taking advantage of the right occasion to wear it."

Phoena retrieved the hat and waited while Nessie put it on. Nessie grabbed Phoena's arm and propelled her from the room. "Come on!"

CHAPTER 3:
FRIEND
OR FOE?

After a rapid descent to the ground floor, they arrived in a broad foyer. Uniformed footmen stood at attention beside the ornately carved doors. Nessie fussed over her reflection in front of a large wall mirror. She took particular care with the brown curls that framed her face. Finally, she nodded to the footmen who swung the doors inward.

"Don't look to the right or the left," Nessie whispered to Phoena as they stepped across the threshold.

Nessie's instruction intensified Phoena's nerves. Straight ahead, at the end of a narrow aisle, the headmistress and her staff were waiting. A glance at the wider room revealed rows of young ladies standing beside their tables. Every head was turned towards the door.

Inside the dining room, a third footman waited to receive them. He held out his gloved hand, and Nessie accepted it as if this was something she did often. When the footman extended the other hand towards Phoena, she blushed as she copied her new friend.

The footman took a step forward. "Lady Cascade and Miss Ashton!"

At the far end of the dining hall, the headmistress stood behind a long table. The teaching staff were arranged like statues on either side of Mrs Hammersley. The footman delivered the girls to a spot in front of the headmistress.

"How good of you to *join us*, Lady Cascade," Mrs Hammersley said with a frown. Nessie grinned and curtseyed in acknowledgement. Then the headmistress turned the same stern glare towards Phoena. "Miss Ashton, this tardiness is disappointing. If you continue in this manner, you will bring dishonour to your guardian." Phoena bowed her head.

The headmistress sat on an elaborate bentwood chair. There was a noisy shuffling as everyone else in the dining hall copied her example.

Phoena followed Nessie towards another table set apart from the student tables. She had not expected to see her godmother here, seated amongst some other ladies. At her previous school, it had been rare for visitors to join the students in the dining hall. Cecily sat with her back straight, a neutral expression on her face. They had discussed the emotional distance society required for women in their situation – it would be easier for Cecily to watch from the sidelines if everyone presumed her interest in her goddaughter was minimal. Therefore, Phoena tried not to read any disapproval in this exchange – yet her uncertainty awakened.

"Ladies," Nessie said, curtseying politely, and Phoena copied her actions. Some of the women at the table smiled. Nessie continued, "Please accept my apology for being late. I pray that you can forgive the inconvenience. I hope that the delay does not prevent you from enjoying your meal."

Phoena squeezed her hands together as they turned back to face the other students. The layout was identical to the dining hall at the *Westernbrooke Academy*. Except there, no student ever apologised for being late.

Every step felt like walking on sharp stones. Facing this whispering assembly was worse than serving a hundred adolescent boys. Phoena wondered if young girls were as prone to mischief as their male counterparts?

The other students were unashamedly staring at her as if she were an exhibit in a zoo. She smiled wryly over memories of familiar scenes from the *Academy* dining hall. They were chased from her memory by her recollection of the final drama that led to her departure from that establishment. One of the senior students, Lord Karilion, had tried using magic to coerce her into a frivolous game. Her resistance captured his attention. But it was her ability to deflect his powerful spell which changed everything.

Before that, Phoena's lowly status had made her the target for many practical jokes. She had even survived some more malicious attacks. Phoena sighed. Cecily had promised her fairer treatment here, but this introduction was not a good start.

Nessie strutted across the room towards two vacant chairs. The other girls watched their approach. Phoena could discern little from their scrutiny.

After Nessie and Phoena sat side by side, the pretty dark-haired girl across the table spoke. "*Miss* Ashton," she said. "We tolerate Lady Cascade at our table because she *is* the oldest student here. Don't think we have to extend the same honour to you. You look terrified, which suggests you're not ready to join *civilised* society. Clearly, you've come from the provinces. You can stay this once. We don't want to humiliate you in front of the whole school. But expect to be reassigned to another table for future meals."

Nessie smiled sweetly. "Oh, shut up, Meredith. You're living proof that there's more to being ready for 'civilised society' than where your family comes from."

Meredith retaliated, an equally sweet expression on her face. "And *you* are evidence that civilised society is wasted on *some* people." She glanced towards her friends for support. "You look the part, but you're only tolerated because of your connections. You'll never amount to anything, and everyone knows it."

A tall crystal water decanter sat in the centre of the table. Nessie nudged it with her fingers. Phoena gasped as Meredith shrieked. The indignant girl leapt to her feet to avoid a stream of water flowing from the overturned vessel. One of the maids hurried forward to mop up the spill.

"Apologies for my clumsiness," Nessie said.

The stockily-built girl on the opposite side of Phoena leaned closer. Her brown shoulder-length hair was unadorned. Her plainness contrasted with the others.

"Welcome to *Quenthlaretta College*," she said in a low voice. "I'm Lady Yiana Yianothalis. Pay no attention to Meredith and the others. Nessie outranks them all, making this her table. If she says you're to sit here, no one can make you move."

CHAPTER 4:
MAGICAL MISCHIEF

While Phoena pushed her food around her plate, she watched the others closely. Meredith and her cohort were ignoring the new girl. Halfway through the first luncheon course, Meredith's left-hand neighbour leaned forward and directed a flash of pink light towards Nessie. The spell fizzed and spun in the air. More than one diner paused to see what the outcome would be.

Then it vanished without a sound.

Nessie continued eating. Had she failed to notice anything? The wide brim of her hat made it impossible to see her face. Phoena could no longer detect any magic – the spell-caster seemed puzzled. What had happened to the spell? Whispered comments passed between Meredith's allies.

A few minutes later, Nessie set down her fork and pushed away her plate. She removed her hat and turned the creation over. After examining it, her fingers pointed to a dark blemish. Nessie brushed at it with her fingers.

Addressing Phoena in a loud voice, Nessie asked, "Did I tell you that the Princess Royal's milliner made my hat?" Everyone at the table froze in their seats. Nessie winked at Phoena. "It has the same magical protections reserved for her. The Princess *will* be pleased when I report her latest innovation works perfectly."

This comment sent a ripple of anxious glances around the table. Meanwhile, Yiana reached for the hat. Without hesitation, Nessie passed it to her.

"I was wondering if you'd noticed anything," Yiana said. "I know you have trouble detecting magic, but you usually have some kind of protection about you."

"What spell was it this time?" Nessie asked, retrieving her hat. She smiled cheerfully across the table, but nobody responded.

"A little persuasion charm," Yiana said. Her green eyes sparkled as she leaned closer to Phoena. "I saw you react as the spell flew across the table. Don't worry. They won't direct anything at you until they work out your defences."

"They should be more worried about whether she knows any spells," Nessie said with a wicked laugh.

Horrified, Phoena fought the urge to kick her companion under the table. A quick reply from across the table shocked her even more.

"This is just a little game we play," Meredith said, smiling at Phoena. "Nessie enjoys showing off, and we're more than *happy* to oblige."

CHAPTER 5:
A SHOCKING CHANGE

Cecily summoned Phoena when the headmistress released the students from the dining room. Her godmother straightened the collar on Phoena's brown dress. "I have packed your favourite mirror, girl – make sure you use it."

Phoena blinked at the reference to this marvellous mirror. Taking her cue from the older woman's formal tone, she bowed her head and dropped into a curtsey. "Yes, Lady Cecily."

"I will send the coach to collect you after dinner."

Her godmother turned away.

Nessie waited until Cecily left the dining room before she seized Phoena's arm and shouted. "Upstairs now!"

"There's just enough time to change before our first lesson," Yiana added. She was broader at the shoulders than at the hips and grabbed the other arm. Arm in arm, the trio stormed the stairs.

"What do we have this afternoon?" Nessie asked, pausing at the first landing.

"Heraldry, followed by Philosophy," Yiana said.

Nessie groaned.

"I tried signing up for the new Defensive Coach Driving course," Yiana said, "but Mama tore up the permission form.

"'A young lady must always employ a coachman if unable to persuade a nobleman to be her driver.' Mama's thinking is *so-o* last century."

Phoena's two companions nattered all the way to the second floor. As they turned towards the third flight of stairs, Nessie stopped again. "You're very quiet, Phoena. Are you still worried about that spell?"

Phoena said the first thing that came into her head. "How did you *know* there was a spell?"

"I felt a vibration here," Nessie said, pointing to her temple. "It only happens when someone uses magic nearby. Today, I also had a buzzing sensation, so I knew the hat was working. I usually rely on Yiana to tell me what kind of spell I've deflected."

"Doesn't it worry you that people are using magic against you?"

"Of course not." Nessie laughed. "This is good preparation for the King's Court. The Princess Royal says little spells are whizzing about all the time there. Sometimes they hit their mark, but more often, some innocent bystander gets caught. A girl must prepare, or she might find herself betrothed to some tedious man."

"Or tricked into a financial alliance that can only end in disaster," Yiana said.

"Or embroiled in a scandal. Imagine having to hide away until some other unfortunate girl does something worse."

Phoena shook her head at their attitude before pressing on with her questions. "Did you see the spell?" she asked Yiana.

"I caught a pink flash," Yiana said. "Sometimes, I can detect magical protections too. There's a humming coming from Nessie today – it must be the hat. That's why I didn't warn her. I knew she was safe."

"Do you know a lot about magic?" Phoena asked. Her head was throbbing, but her curiosity was more insistent than her apprehension.

"There are lots of magic users in my family," Yiana replied. "On a rare occasion, the talent comes to a woman. I've missed out, but that doesn't mean I must remain ignorant of the possibilities. I have access to my father's extensive library, and I can identify most of the spells that the apothecaries sell."

"Today's spell wasn't the first one the Inner Circle have tried," Nessie said, "and I'd be disappointed if it was the last. I keep hoping one of them tries a growth spell. I've always wanted to be taller." She raised her hand high above her head. "I hate being mistaken for a child."

"Then you should stop acting like one." Yiana laughed. "You'll be waiting forever for that kind of spell. None of the girls here would purchase anything that caused a permanent change."

"At the *Westernbrooke Academy*," Nessie said, "there was a foreign nobleman who grew. I've heard whispers, but nobody will confirm the details. If I could find out what spell he used, I'd offer up half my fortune to have it."

"That wasn't a spell," Yiana said. "That was powerful magic."

The star-shaped scar on Phoena's forearm burned as a reminder of danger. She stumbled, almost falling in her haste to disentangle herself from the others. Her companions helped her regain her balance, staring when she tried to shake off their hands.

She freed herself from Yiana's grasp, but Nessie hooked her left arm around Phoena's waist.

"You've gone pale," Nessie said. "Nobody here can do real magic, so there's nothing for you to worry about."

As Nessie held her close, a surge of pain ran along Phoena's arm.

"I'm not worried about me," Phoena whispered, raising a hand to her throat as her eyes closed. Through the fabric, she could feel the metal medallion. "Baraapa didn't ask to be taller—"

"Hey!" shouted Nessie.

The darkness faltered. Phoena's cheek was stinging.

"Nessie!" cried Yiana. "You don't slap someone who's fainting."

"She wasn't fainting!" Nessie said from the upper step. "She was about to transport herself out of here. I may not have any magic, but I've seen Karil escape from enough tricky situations to recognise the signs. I couldn't let her leave without explaining what she meant."

Phoena opened her eyes to see a dazzling blue cloud encircling them. A groan erupted from Phoena's throat, and her stomach cramped.

Not again! A supernatural light leapt between Phoena and Nessie before shooting upwards towards the remarkable hat.

Kaboom!

With a blinding flash, the hat blasted into the air.

Whoosh!

It flew up the stairs and disappeared around the corner.

Yiana stifled a scream.

Nessie sat on the step with a loud thump.

"I'll get help," Yiana said, turning first towards the upper level and then back towards the way they had come. There were tears in her eyes.

"Wait," cried Nessie. "Whatever happened is almost done. Help me up."

Yiana hauled Nessie upright while Phoena retreated even further.

"How are we going to explain this?" Yiana wailed.

"Explain what?" Nessie asked. "Am I taller?"

"No-o," Yiana said, her eyes wide. "But your hair..."

"What about my hair?" Nessie cried, tugging at the ribbons. The hair tumbled loose, a fountain of iridescent blue flowing over her shoulders.

"I've never seen that colour before," Yiana said. "Your hair reminds me of the river on a summer's day, bright blue with the sunlight flickering on the surface."

Nessie shrieked with delight. "I've been magicked! And neither of us saw it coming! Oh, what fun!"

Yiana shook her head. "I'm more worried about how long it will last."

"I hope it's permanent." Nessie continued to celebrate. "What excuse will we use? We can't let anyone know that Phoena did this. Life would become impossible for her—"

"Don't worry about me," Phoena said. The other girls made no reply, lost to their problem-solving. Phoena sat down, resting her chin in her hands.

A wavering smile replaced Yiana's frown. "We could tell them there was a delay with the earlier spell."

"I don't think they'd believe that," Nessie said.

"Or the hat malfunctioned–"

"No, the Princess Royal would order an investigation."

"We could say that someone left a spell on the stairs–"

"Or I purchased another spell, and it misfired. It wouldn't be the first time."

Phoena stared at the pair in disbelief. The light coming through the narrow window made Nessie's blue hair shine. The silvery flashes triggered another memory. Phoena's power usually spirited her away to a dark cavern beside an underground river. The reflected light on Nessie's hair acted like the silvered fishes that darted beneath the waves. She recalled Nessie's earlier offer to be her champion, and trembled. The tingling in Phoena's hands warned her that the supernatural power within her hadn't finished yet.

"Hey!" a voice called from above. "Is Nessie looking for her hat?"

The hat sailed down towards them. Yiana snatched it from the air. Nessie bundled her hair on top of her head and pulled on the hat. The pair worked together to conceal every blue strand.

"Don't worry," Nessie said to Phoena as she dragged her upright. "Everyone will assume I've done this to myself. Crazy things happen around me *all* the time."

The tingling intensified, but the power seemed content with this preliminary mischief.

"Or they'll think she's 'showing off'," Yiana said, in an acceptable imitation of Meredith's sarcastic tone. She ran up the remaining stairs ahead of them. "We're fortunate Nessie chose today for such a large hat."

At the top of the stairs, Yiana hesitated. "I forgot to ask – have I changed?"

Nessie paused and studied her. "I don't think so. You look the same." She turned to Phoena. "Has anything happened to Yiana?"

Phoena shook her head. "The energy targeted you."

"Oh well." Yiana shrugged. "That's one complication I don't have to factor in." She stepped into the hallway. "I don't know if I'm relieved or disappointed."

"I'm sure we could ask Phoena–" Nessie began.

Yiana leapt back in alarm. "No! They'll believe anything about you, Nessie, but if something happened to me–"

"I think the hat saved you," Nessie said. "It pulled all the magic towards me. But if you tell Phoena what you want–"

"It doesn't work like that," Phoena said.

"How does it work, then?"

"I'm not sure. I'm still learning. The theory is that I'm a catalyst. When something happens, the person affected is always touching me." Phoena flinched as the memory of being carried by Viscount Baraapa flooded her being. His transformation had been dramatic. The power within her changed him from a scrawny teenager into a mighty mountain of muscles with copper coloured skin. His hair had turned a vibrant orange.

"But something different happens each time. It's almost as if the power determines the outcome."

"So why did your magic think Nessie needed blue hair?" Yiana asked.

Looking along the hallway, Phoena frowned at the potential witnesses. Students were coming and going from each other's rooms.

Nessie nodded. "Quick, into my room."

CHAPTER 6:
THE FIRST CHALLENGE

In the classroom, there were twelve chairs arranged in a semi-circle around a raised dais. The three vacant chairs were right in front of the master. Phoena hated being late, but Nessie delighted in another opportunity for a grand entrance. This time, Nessie wore a voluminous headscarf attached to a cone-shaped cap.

The Heraldry Master stood on a raised platform. The middle-aged man peered over the top of his spectacles. "Lady Cascade," he grumbled, "I did not request anyone to appear in period costume."

A ripple of laughter ran around the room, and he turned his stern glare towards the other girls. "Can anyone tell us which epoch Lady Cascade has referenced in her headdress?"

Nessie grinned at Phoena as an uncomfortable silence fell.

Yiana rose to her feet. "The Second Impress Dynasty, during the reign of the Dowager Queen Irindruk. The Queen suffered from hair loss and favoured headscarves to hide her baldness. Her ladies-in-waiting adopted the same fashion. During the Queen's reign, no civilised woman appeared in public with her hair uncovered. The ladies of the Court devised an array of pointy caps with attached veils, called *hennin*. The *hennin* distinguished them from the lesser nobility."

"And made them look taller," Nessie added. The other girls laughed.

"Humph!" Master Fitzgibbons muttered.

For the next half an hour, he reviewed two hundred heraldic symbols in contemporary use. He used a long swishy stick to point to the designs on a series of posters behind him. He said everyone would take part, yet he called on Nessie or Yiana to answer most of the questions. Phoena was only asked to identify three. She was both surprised and relieved that she answered correctly.

"There are only twelve of you in this senior class," the Master said. "You should each be able to identify your family shield." He walked to the side and dragged across a large display board on wheels. There were eight heraldic shields on display. "But have you the knowledge and skills to identify unfamiliar standards without assistance? That is the question that you are to ask yourself each week. Which of you knows the family represented by the first one?" He pointed to the upper left standard.

"That's easy," said Meredith. "That's the King's ensign."

"Does everyone agree?" Master Fitzgibbons asked. The other girls affirmed that answer. The process continued until there was only one standard remaining to identify. It featured a black fire-breathing dragon on a red field with a plain gold border. The design seemed simplistic in comparison to the others.

A hush fell. The Master turned to Yiana. "Why is this one more difficult to identify?"

"This is foreign," Yiana said.

"I'm sure I've seen it recently," Nessie added. "So it must have been on display in the capital? Perhaps over an estate rented by a foreign ambassador?"

After some unsuccessful guesses, even Yiana and Nessie confessed their ignorance. Phoena leaned forward. What would be the consequences if she gave the answer? Her hand slipped into her pocket. This morning, there hadn't been time to read the letter from Oramis. The Master must have noticed her movement.

"Miss Ashton, if you have a suggestion, you should speak up," he said. "This establishment is not the place for lazy girls who leave all the work to their betters."

Nessie opened her mouth, but Phoena silenced her with a small gesture. Master Fitzgibbons folded his arms and tapped his foot.

Phoena cleared her throat. "You said–" Her voice squeaked, and she tried again. "You said we weren't to speak if we had a personal connection with the family represented."

"And *you* have a connection with *this* family?" he asked.

Phoena nodded.

His frown deepened. "I'm still waiting for your guardian to provide me with the necessary information. Even so, I'm prepared to wager that you aren't a member of this family."

"No, I'm not," Phoena replied. "But I have received letters that bear this seal."

"Why would the Emberite Ambassador be writing to *you*?" Master Fitzgibbons asked, and then he clamped his jaws shut. "Humph!" he said and turned towards the clock.

"This class is dismissed." He left the room before any of the girls rose from their seats.

Phoena followed Nessie and Yiana, who held themselves apart from the other girls. Nessie waited until they were alone in the hallway before she started to giggle.

"Why *would* the Emberite Ambassador be writing to you?" Nessie asked, and her hand stole the letter out of Phoena's pocket. "I remember meeting him, and he didn't seem the type to be corresponding with young ladies. But he does have two sons..."

Yiana leaned closer, and together they studied the seal. "Stop teasing Phoena," Yiana said, passing the letter back to Phoena. It disappeared into her pocket. "I'm more interested in some of the other things Fitzgibbons said."

"Well, I didn't like his tone," Nessie said. "Fitzgibbons was sure that none of us would know the final answer. I'm hoping Phoena shows him up again next week."

CHAPTER 7:
MISTAKES AND MISUNDERSTANDINGS

"You've survived your first lessons," Nessie said as she towed Phoena along the hallway. Yiana had gone to her own room in the opposite wing. "I thought you were in trouble when Madame Devinette asked you that hard question. How did you remember the names of the original Elemental Fellowship champions? I always get them muddled, and you even managed to match them to their elemental talents. Yiana's the only one I've ever heard answer that question to Madame's satisfaction."

"I have an advantage," Phoena said. "I've spent time with people who believe this is important history, not a fanciful story."

"Is it true that Lady de Montnoir is a member of the Fellowship?"

Phoena pretended not to hear. "Here's your room." She prepared to walk on, but Nessie took her by the arm. Her voice dropped to a whisper. "I bet you're a member of the Fellowship too! Stop frowning at me; it makes you look ancient and forbidding. I'm two years your senior, and I don't want you to forget that." Nessie laughed as she pushed open her door. She didn't give Phoena time to protest. Her voice rose to her usual volume. "Now help me decide what I'm going to wear this evening."

Meredith stood near a low table in the centre of the reception room. Phoena counted the cups and saucers. The table was set for half a dozen guests.

"That will be all, Daisy," Meredith said, addressing the maid. The servant swung the kettle over the fire in the grate before bowing and disappearing from the room.

As soon as the door closed, Meredith stormed across to her cousin. She attempted to use her height as an advantage, but Nessie would have none of it. Nessie still held Phoena's arm as if to use her as a shield. Phoena straightened, realising that she was taller than Meredith.

Fifteen-year-old Meredith frowned. "I told you to spend your afternoon with Yiana," she said to Nessie. "You know it's my turn to host the Inner Circle for afternoon tea. We *agreed* you would make yourself absent."

"This is *my* apartment, and I come and go as I please," Nessie replied. Her quiet tone did not match her fingers which squeezed Phoena's tingling arm. She nudged Nessie in warning but received only a wink in reply. Nessie smiled cheerfully at Meredith. "Don't worry. I'm here to collect a few things, and then I'm going to Phoena's suite."

Now, it was Phoena's turn to receive Meredith's displeasure. The younger girl's face contorted into an unflattering expression. Phoena had last seen that kind of look when Cecily found an unwelcome slug in her salad.

Meredith's voice sent a chill down Phoena's spine. "I don't understand why you're spending so much time with this new girl. She's an outsider, and there's nothing to be gained from cultivating her friendship."

"I have my reasons," Nessie said, pulling Phoena into her bedroom and slamming the door. "I'd apologise for my cousin, but her kind of prejudice is more common than I'd like to admit."

After taking a deep breath, Phoena replied. "I'm used to being the 'outsider'." Nessie stood still for the longest time. In the silence, Phoena's heart pounded, and her face became flushed.

Finally, Nessie broke the stalemate. She flounced across to the dressing table and removed the hennin from her head. She smiled at her reflection in the mirror. "Is that all you have to say?"

Nessie shook her blue hair loose. She rushed to a line drawn on the doorpost and leaned against the mark. "Are you sure I'm not taller?"

Phoena shook her head, hiding her tingling hands behind her back.

Nessie narrowed her eyes.

With a sigh, Nessie opened the wardrobe and pulled out a dress. After holding the garment under her chin, Nessie shook her head.

The rejected dress flew towards the bed. This process continued until there was a big mound of discarded dresses. When the weight was too great, the whole stack slithered onto the floor.

Phoena gathered the colourful dresses in her arms to return them to the bed.

Meanwhile, Nessie danced around the room with a dark blue dress before her. "This goes so well with my hair," she laughed. Phoena replaced a dress on a hanger and took it to the wardrobe.

Nessie ignored her. Instead, she rummaged through another cupboard for matching shoes and a hat.

"Leave that for the maid," Nessie said, when she was through with her choosing.

"Why should I leave for the maid something I can do for myself?"

"Because that's what maids are for."

"Don't you think the maids have more than enough to do?" Phoena asked. She continued the task until all the dresses were away. She then turned towards the loose shoes scattered across the floor.

Nessie stomped her foot. "If you're so eager to serve, you can carry this." She thrust a bag into Phoena's hands.

The insult was too much for Phoena. She took half a step back. The sudden discomfort in her stomach reminded her of the last time someone punched her. The star-shaped scar on her arm burned, and the sparks at her fingertips were a warning.

Her power didn't like being bossed around. Phoena turned her back on her new friend, snatched up the bag and rushed to the door.

When Nessie appeared beside her, the headscarf covered the blue hair again. She carried the dark blue dress she had chosen. Neither of them said anything. They crossed the reception room, ignoring Meredith's glare. They made it to Phoena's suite without any further word.

Yiana was waiting outside Phoena's door, clutching a battered leather-bound book. A yellow dress hung over one arm, and a closed bag sat on the floor. She frowned, glancing from Phoena to Nessie. Phoena shuffled her feet, but Nessie shrugged.

"I thought we could try these recipes," Yiana said in a loud voice. Some girls further up the corridor snickered. "I'm sure Phoena won't mind if we use her rooms for our experiments."

Nessie opened the suite door. Phoena picked up Yiana's bag and carried it with Nessie's bag into the room. She dropped both bags onto a chair and folded her arms across her chest. "What experiments?" Phoena asked as the door closed.

"Don't worry," Yiana said. "We're only pretending. I've sent one of the servants off to the apothecary with a long list of ingredients. I've also sent for some pots to boil up our potions."

Phoena reached for the dark blue dress.

Nessie stiffened, but then she passed the garment across. Before she released her hold, Nessie stared into Phoena's eyes. "I apologise," Nessie said. "It was embarrassing watching you tidy up after me as if you were my servant. And I'm annoyed that I'm still short. I hoped you might react – but I realise now that I've made a terrible mistake."

"I accept your apology," Phoena said. She reached for Yiana's dress. It was a relief to escape to the dressing room. When Phoena returned, Nessie and Yiana were in earnest conversation.

"I know you've worked hard on this plan," Nessie said, "but what if someone checks the book and knows it's the wrong kind of spell—"

"The book is obsolete." Yiana sounded impatient. She strode to the fireplace. The fire had burned low, but there were still a few glowing coals. "Papa ordered it removed from his library. I sneaked it away for such an emergency as this." She opened the book and flipped it upside down. Yiana tossed the entire volume onto the fire and walked away without a second glance. "We'll tell them the accident destroyed the book."

Phoena watched in horror as the heavy parchment smouldered within the flames. Billowing black smoke filled the fireplace. It took only a few seconds for the fumes to start drifting into the room. Even from the other side of the room, the horrible stench was impossible to ignore. Didn't these noblewomen understand the consequences of their foolish actions!

Yiana turned, but nothing in her stance showed any great concern. "Bother! There's not enough heat left for the book to burn properly. I'll have to call a maid—"

"Don't," Nessie said to Yiana. "I didn't get a chance to tell you. Phoena knows all about fires. She can fix this."

Even as she rushed towards the fireplace, Phoena wrestled with a difficult decision. Her godmother had forbidden her from using her powers in front of witnesses. But if she did nothing, this mess would render her apartment uninhabitable. It might take days for the servants to get rid of the smoke stains and this foul smell.

Glancing towards the older teenagers, she made her decision. "Close all the doors to keep the smoke in this room. Then go into the pantry and organise the tea things. I'll deal with this."

Nessie led Yiana away. As soon as they were out of the room, Phoena covered her nose with her skirt and bent down. The stench made her gag. She closed her watering eyes and imagined a small dragon blowing flames at the book.

Whoosh! Within seconds, crackling flames engulfed the book. A glorious fire now roared in the grate and a vigorous updraft drew the smoke up the chimney.

Phoena took a step back to protect her dress from the

increasing inferno. After she waved her hand toward the flames, the fire settled into a calmer blaze.

Satisfied, Phoena tossed more fuel on the fire and probed it with the poker to hasten the book's demise. The burning book sizzled and hissed. Now that the object was completely alight, Phoena rushed to the window and threw it open. The fresh air was welcome.

With a swish of her hand, Phoena summoned a strong breeze to sweep away the foul-smelling fumes. She waved her hand, and a gentle mist filled the space and then drifted out the window.

For a moment, she imagined her dragon-friend hovering outside the window. She blinked, and the illusion was gone. Phoena enjoyed the fresh-rain fragrance that replaced the smoke.

A polished kettle hung on a hook beside the fireplace. Phoena lifted the lid and saw that it was empty. With another wave of her hand, a small raincloud appeared over the kettle. The pitter-patter of gentle rain soothed Phoena's nerves.

When the kettle was full, she clicked her fingers and dismissed the cloud. It floated out the window. Phoena hung the kettle over the flames, adjusting the position by resting her hands on the metal.

The temperature of her hands rivalled the heat from the fire. A fine mist began to rise from the kettle spout. Phoena smiled. It was satisfying to see that she was learning to manage her new skills.

A small clatter was her only warning that Nessie and Yiana were returning. How much had they seen?

Nessie gave her no time to ask. "Oh, good! You've already put the kettle on. Let's go and choose your evening dress while we wait for the water to boil."

A surprise greeted Phoena in the dressing room. Both her heavy trunks had disappeared, and her clothes were in the cupboards. She felt ashamed – unpacking would have been a lengthy task. Nessie opened the wardrobe doors, talking to herself as she ran her hands along the garments. Meanwhile, Yiana went to the dressing table and picked up a mirror in an ornate gilded frame.

"Is this what I *think* it is?" Yiana asked. There was an eagerness in her tone that Phoena hadn't heard before.

Nessie skipped over and snatched it from Yiana. "Is this a magic mirror?" Nessie laughed at her reflection on the silvered surface. "Mirror, mirror, speak to me. Show me what I need to see!"

"Don't!" Yiana cried.

"Stop!" Phoena shouted.

"There's no need to yell at me," Nessie said, her lips pouting.

"Lady Nessandra Cascade," a stern voice said from the mirror. "There had better be a good reason for your summons."

Yiana caught the mirror as Nessie leapt backwards. Phoena took it from the plump girl's trembling hands. Cecily's face shone from within the frame as if her godmother was a living portrait.

"I apologise, Cecily," Phoena said. "I've tried to be careful, but Nessie keeps provoking a reaction, and I'm having trouble controlling my power."

Yiana gasped. Phoena straightened her shoulders and

refocused her smile.

"Indeed," Cecily replied. "I sensed as much when I saw her this morning. More trouble, but with your history, that's not unexpected. You seem to have picked up another conspirator. Is that one of Paulo Yianothalis's daughters I see beside you?"

"Y-yes." The plump girl was shaking. "Yiana Yianothalis at your service, Lady de M-Montnoir." She dropped into an awkward curtsey.

"Find somewhere to hang the mirror," Cecily commanded. "I want to see all three of you at the same time."

Phoena surveyed the room. Nessie rushed towards a wall where a large floral painting had prime position. Yiana helped her lift down the massive artwork.

"Why did you pick this huge painting," Yiana muttered. "It's only a small mirror."

"I'm sure this location is perfect," Nessie said as they leaned the painting against another wall. Phoena sighed. Starting another discussion about creating extra work for the servants was counterproductive. A surge of energy flowed through her arms. She tucked the mirror under her arm for safekeeping and gestured towards the demounted painting. It quivered for a moment and then shrank to a smaller size. She raised her hand, and the framed canvas floated over to the wall beside the door. After it attached itself to the wall at eye level, Phoena smiled, and her confidence surged.

Next, Phoena launched the mystical mirror towards the wall behind Nessie and Yiana. The precious object arced towards the floor and Yiana choked on a scream. The mirror wavered and then rose into the air. As it approached its destination, the mirror grew. Nessie pulled Yiana out of the way. The mirror hung itself, now dominating the room as if it had always been there. It was the perfect size.

"I told you," Nessie said, her hands on her hips.

"There's no need to look so smug," Cecily said. She was life-sized now, appearing as if she might step through into the dressing room. Cecily towered over the three teenagers. Nessie's diminutive height became an obvious disadvantage, causing her to hasten towards Phoena.

"Are you going to come through the mirror?" Nessie asked.

"Everything necessary can be accomplished from this side," Cecily replied. "Receiving you as candidates is only a formality. Lord Westernbrooke and Lady Ennallya will serve as the official witnesses."

"Candidates!" Yiana squeaked. She half-turned towards the exit.

"Yiana, don't be a goose," Nessie said. "Between us, we've faced more intimidating interviews than this. We haven't done anything wrong."

"Nessie," Yiana hissed. "If you had any common sense, you'd keep quiet. Don't you know who Lord Westernbrooke and Lady Ennallya are?"

"Of course I do," Nessie said. "Lord Westernbrooke founded the *Westernbrooke Academy*. And Lady Ennallya is part of the legend about the Elemental Fellowsh– Oh!" The colour drained from her face.

"Lady de Montnoir said we were candidates," Yiana said.

"But that means–"

Nessie fainted, and Yiana caught her just in time.

CHAPTER 8:
UNPREPARED CANDIDATES

Phoena's godfather Lord Westernbrooke strode into view within the mirror. His long white beard flowed down his heavy burgundy robes. Too big to stand upright and fit within the mirror's frame, he sat in a chair. Cecily patted his arm. She was a tall woman, but her head was at the level of his, even when seated. When he had settled, she gestured for a smaller woman to join them. Ennallya was centuries older than the other guardians, but her grey hair was the only hint of her age.

"Can you see all three of us?" Cecily asked.

Phoena nodded. "Can you see us?"

"Of course," Lord Westernbrooke's booming voice filled her dressing-room. Phoena's companions drew closer to her. Nessie had regained consciousness a few moments after her fainting spell but remained pale. Yiana had her arm around Nessie's waist to support her.

"What have you told these candidates?" Lord Westernbrooke asked.

"I haven't told them anything," Phoena said. "I didn't realise they were candidates. Nessie said the trigger phrase and the mirror did the rest."

Lord Westernbrooke frowned at Cecily. "It's happened again. Candidates without any understanding of the commitment they are about to undertake."

Cecily placed her hand on his arm. "You forget that you were once like them. This requires a certain courage only found in the young." Her hand pointed towards Phoena's side of the mirror, and she smiled. "The elemental power has drawn these two young ladies to their nomination. It is not our role to question their suitability."

"The one with the blue hair has potential, but I sense no magical energy around the other one," he grumbled.

Yiana seemed to shrink at this comment, but Nessie's smile strengthened. Phoena leaned closer to Yiana. "You'll get used to his manner," Phoena whispered. "He hasn't seen any redeeming features in the other candidates either. I'm not even sure he approves of me."

Cecily addressed Lord Westernbrooke. "Don't be too hasty in your assessment, Westy," she said with a crooked smile. "I don't think Phoena's talent has finished its work."

"Why not? Her transformative power isn't known for its restraint."

"I sense that your goddaughter did everything she could to prevent this nomination."

He glared at Phoena, but she offered no reply. She was busy praying, her restless power an uncomfortable distraction. She shuffled further away to spare Yiana any complications.

"It was my fault," Nessie said, shaking off Yiana's arm. She straightened to her full height and approached the mirror. Nessie stopped when she was almost near enough to touch it. "I provoked Phoena into reacting, and then I wouldn't let her go." Her chin lifted as she boldly matched Lord Westernbrooke's stare. "Her magic lashed out at me and blasted my protections into oblivion. I have only one regret – that I didn't remove the protections myself. I've never felt more alive, and I can assure you that I'm more than ready for her to hit me with her magic again."

"I hope you don't come to regret that invitation. Phoena's gifts come with high expectations – and even greater responsibilities." He paused, pulling on his beard. "Lady Nessandra Cascade; I have known three generations of your family. Perhaps there is something beneath your reckless pride that might redeem you." He dismissed her with a wave of his hand. Nessie backed away until she rejoined Yiana.

"And the other girl?" Lord Westernbrooke asked Cecily. "A Yianothalis? One of Paulo's brood? He's not mentioned a talented daughter. How did she escape Phoena's magic?"

"She can speak for herself," Cecily replied. "Lady Yiana, please come closer."

Yiana nodded. After inhaling deeply, she lifted her head. Slowly, she walked towards the mirror until she reached the spot where Nessie had stood. Then the plump teenager dropped into a deep curtsey before rising to face him. Lord Westernbrooke lifted his hand in a silent invitation.

"My Lord, I can detect magic," Yiana said, "but I have no talent of my own. I knew enough to keep my distance when Phoena's magic activated."

Ennallya spoke for the first time. "Common sense and a touch of wisdom far outweigh a mountain of mystical talent." A silence followed her gentle words.

"Indeed," Lord Westernbrooke said. He studied Yiana for a few minutes. When she said nothing further, he waved his hand. Hastily retreating, Yiana rejoined Nessie. Lord Westernbrooke stretched his hand sideways. "Pass me my staff. It is time for these girls to make their decision." Cecily handed him a long wooden pole topped with a bird-like silver ornament. He tapped the base on the floor.

"Candidates, you have been nominated." His words echoed around the dressing room, growing as if they had their own power. "The choice to accept or reject this nomination is yours alone." He paused and glared at them. "I caution you to take careful consideration before you make your decision."

"Of course, we accept!" Nessie said, bouncing on the spot. "Yes, yes, yes! I've always wanted to tell everyone that I belong to a secret society."

Phoena moved sideways to study the responses of her new friends. She tore her eyes from the jubilant Nessie, glancing towards the mirror. Lord Westernbrooke seemed unchanged, but the other guardians smiled.

Yiana groaned as she put out a constraining hand. "The whole point of a 'secret society' is not to tell anyone."

Nessie pouted. The smaller teenager opened her mouth, and Yiana shook her head. An unspoken exchange passed between them. Nessie stopped her protest, and a charming smile replaced her consternation. Yiana faced the mirror again. "You said that this is an important decision," she said. "I have some questions before I give you my answer."

"And so you should," Lord Westernbrooke said. "Ask."

"You have neglected to tell us the details of this nomination. I can only assume that the three of you are here as representatives for the Elemental Fellowship?"

"Yes."

"The same Fellowship which supported the five champions centuries ago?"

"Indeed, although more than five were involved in that victory. The other champions chose to remain anonymous."

"And a new group of champions is currently being recruited?"

"So it would seem."

Yiana rested her chin in her hand.

Perhaps this was a prearranged signal because Nessie winked at Phoena as she stepped forward. "Why now?"

Lord Westernbrooke shifted in his chair. He conferred silently with his companions. Cecily nodded, but it was Ennallya who answered. "There has been a continuous line of elemental champions since the beginning. Many of them have accepted their role without being required to do anything heroic. The other members of the Fellowship serve to guide and protect the champions.

Nessie smiled. "When do we meet the other members?"

"Those members already in your circle of acquaintance will contact you."

"How many members are there?"

"Enough."

"That's not an answer," Nessie huffed. "What does the Fellowship do?"

"We maintain the peace within the Kingdoms and watch."

Nessie frowned. She walked back towards Yiana, who spoke again. "Why the secrecy?"

Lord Westernbrooke leaned forward. "There have been those who would compel the champions to serve them."

"Ah," Yiana said. She paced backwards and forwards.

Phoena shuffled her feet. The room seemed to shrink. Without realising it, Phoena moved closer to the mirror. Her pulse pounded in her veins.

Nessie disrupted the silence. "How long has Phoena been a member?"

It felt as if everyone held their breath for the answer.

"Since the day she was born," Ennallya said. Her face testified to a deeper sadness. "But that knowledge was withheld from her."

"The Fellowship voted to keep her existence hidden," Lord Westernbrooke said to Ennallya. "It was agreed that her identity and location should be a closely guarded secret."

"But was it necessary to deny her any knowledge of her birthright?"

Phoena had never heard Ennallya raise her voice before.

"This is neither the time nor the place for this discussion," Cecily said.

"I disagree," Ennallya replied. "I believe this has everything to do with what is happening here. These candidates were chosen by her elemental power – the very power that the Fellowship wanted to keep hidden from her."

"It was for her benefit," Lord Westernbrooke muttered.

"What benefit? We left her friendless and alone–"

"She wasn't alone," Cecily cried. "I watched over her. I did what was necessary to protect her."

"But she never knew you were there to protect her," Ennallya said, her voice full of emotion. "Without her power to comfort her, there was no hope of redemption. How long would we have let this continue? Would we ever have released her from bondage?"

"Why would anyone bind her magic?" Nessie demanded.

The guardians in the mirror refocused their attention. Lord Westernbrooke shifted in his chair, frowning from the mirror. "It was the only way to ensure her safety. Of course, we would have informed her – when she was old enough..."

"Did her magic break out and free her?" Nessie demanded.

"There was a gradual awakening," Cecily admitted. "It's too early to determine how strong she will become."

"Why did you bring her here?" Nessie asked. "And what does her magic want with us?"

"Shh, Nessie," Yiana said, placing her hand on her friend's arm. "I've made my decision." Then she carefully dropped to her knees before Phoena.

"Why are we kneel–" Nessie asked.

Yiana shook her head and gestured downward with her hand. Nessie blinked and then copied her friend. "Phoena," Yiana said. "I pledge to serve your noble cause as one of your champions. No matter what the cost."

Phoena reached out her hand and touched Yiana's head. A surge of power flowed between them. Yiana gave no visible indication that she sensed anything. There was no time to ask any questions because Nessie was reaching for Phoena's hand.

"That goes for me too," Nessie said. She leapt to her feet and threw her arms around Phoena. "And please tell your magic I'm ready for whatever it wants to throw at me."

"Ah-hum!" Lord Westernbrooke muttered. The girls turned towards him. Both Nessie and Yiana had their arms around Phoena's waist, moving her to the middle of their huddle. "The nominations have been received and accepted," he said. "Welcome to the Elemental Fellowship. You are to remain together until your services are required."

"Now we will leave you," Cecily said from the mirror as the vision faded. "I am sure you have much to discuss."

"Whoo-hoo!" Nessie shouted. "The three of us are going to have so much fun. I can't wait to see your other magic."

"There will be time for that later," Yiana said. "Our first priority is to find a believable explanation for your blue hair."

Nessie laughed. "I'm sure you'll come up with something. Listen! There's a knock at the door. What perfect timing!" She skipped from the room. "That will be your delivery."

CHAPTER 9:
AN UNFORSEEN COMPLICATION

Two hours later, the three companions were crammed into a room in the first-floor Infirmary. Phoena struggled with Nessie's deception that her dilemma had been caused by an exploding potion rather than a deliberate act. But Yiana was enjoying the unfolding melodrama. Nessie sat in bed, with the covers tucked firmly around her waist. The stern nurse was scrubbing Nessie's exposed skin with a coarse brush.

"Doesn't that hurt?" Phoena whispered to Yiana.

"No," Yiana said. "Nurse Nancy's using a magic brush that only attacks the dye."

"It doesn't seem to be working."

Yiana snorted. Phoena went to the window and stared down at the garden. She thought she detected movement at the edge of her vision. But when she turned her head, there was nothing to see.

"Stop laughing at me," Nessie said, struggling to control her giggles. Phoena glanced towards the bed. Nessie's treatment had lasted for more than twenty minutes. "Can't you see that I'm in a *terrible* state?" Nessie's face and hands were blue.

"You have only yourself to blame," Yiana replied, choking on her laughter. "Nobody told you to toss that blue potion all over yourself."

"I did not!" She looked as if she would launch herself out of bed. The nurse held her still. Nessie pushed her away impatiently, pointing towards Yiana with her stained fingers. "She knows the potion exploded in my face!" Nessie doubled over with another giggling fit. "And now I'm blue."

"This is no laughing matter," Nurse Nancy muttered, rising to her feet. "You're lucky you didn't seriously injure yourself!" She seized the basin of tinted water and gathered up the mound of blue-stained towels. "Lady Cascade, there is nothing more I can do. I dare not scrub your skin anymore."

"Then I can leave!" Nessie said, throwing off the covers.

"Certainly not!" Nurse Nancy said, shoving her back into bed. "Mrs Hammersley has ordered me to keep you here and has authorised a containment spell. You won't be leaving this room until your complexion matches your portrait in her office."

"I don't see why I have to be in the Infirmary," Nessie complained. "I'm not sick."

"You're blue!" Nurse Nancy cried. "And none of you can tell me what was in the potion."

"I have the shopping list," Yiana said, pretending to be contrite. Phoena remained a silent observer.

"If only one of you had saved the book," Nessie said, "instead of fussing over me."

"You're the one who tossed it on the fire when the potion–"

"Enough!" Nurse Nancy said. "Out, out, out! Lady Cascade needs her rest." Nessie poked out her tongue as the nurse shooed Yiana and Phoena from the room. "And don't try the window," the nurse told Nessie. "The charm covers that too."

"Come on, Phoena," said Yiana. "We still have to change for dinner. I can't wait to hear the gossip about Nessie's latest escapade. Didn't she make a glorious fuss as the footman carried her from your suite? Anyone would think she was mortally wounded."

Back on their floor, they hurried to Phoena's room. Phoena matched Yiana stride for stride. Upon arrival, Yiana threw open the door. A team of servants were scrubbing the carpet in front of the fireplace. The brickwork was already clean. Removing the blue dye from the thick woollen carpet was a more difficult task. One of the women leapt to her feet. "I'm sorry, Miss, but we haven't been able to remove the stain."

Phoena recognised the flash of fear this servant tried to conceal. An answering desire to compensate for their failure gave her new energy. "Thank you for your diligence," Phoena said. "You may leave now." She walked to the door and waited while they gathered their equipment.

Before she dismissed them, Phoena extracted a coin purse from her pocket. The women watched her closely. She was confident, despite having no first-hand experience about this kind of exchange. During her years of servitude, she had witnessed many similar transactions.

With deliberate slowness, Phoena counted out four silver coins. She had their full attention now as they lined up at the door. When she placed a coin in each servant's hand, Phoena paused as if she was memorising their faces. One by one, each maid concealed her new riches in her hand, curtsied and waited for her command. "You are to tell the housekeeper that I am satisfied with your work," Phoena said. "I am certain that this is only a temporary spell, and the carpet requires no further attention."

The servants hurried from the room, a mixture of relief and bemusement on their faces. Yiana waited in the middle of the reception room while Phoena closed the door.

"Nessie said you're weird about having servants," Yiana said. "Why did you give them silver? They get paid for the work they do here."

"You paid the servants who delivered your equipment," Phoena said, moving to the hearth to prod the fire.

"That was different," Yiana said. She didn't sound as confident as she usually did. "I paid them to reinforce the idea that Nessie and I were making mischief. And I only gave them bronze coins."

"Was it wrong for me to pay them for trying to clean up *after* your mischief?" Phoena turned and knelt beside the ruined carpet. The scrubbing had only spread the blue stain on the cream coloured carpet.

"Can you fix it?" Yiana asked, kneeling beside her.

"Go and get changed," Phoena said. "I don't like people watching me."

"Is that why you sent us to the pantry before you cleared the smoke from the room? We were watching you through a crack in the door. I had to haul Nessie back when you conjured water from nowhere. Nessie and water have a love-hate relationship."

"What do you mean?"

"She adores the river, but whenever she gets too close, she falls in. Her cousin Karil says she could pretend to be a water sprite if she didn't sink like a stone."

"You asked why my power turned her hair the colour of the river," Phoena said. "You already know the answer. My talent enhances elemental gifts."

"Even if the recipient doesn't have a gift?"

"Especially if the recipient doesn't *know* they have a gift."

"You tried to stop Nessie," Yiana said. "You tried to keep her from holding on to you. What would your magic have gifted me if I hadn't let go?"

"You already know that answer, too," Phoena said. "I can see energy flashing around you. I'm certain you felt the surge of power when I accepted your pledge."

Yiana nodded and grinned. "How long were you a servant at *Westernbrooke Academy?*"

Phoena leapt to her feet. "Who told you that?"

"Shh," Yiana said, grasping Phoena's arm to keep her from fleeing. "I was guessing, but your reaction is confirmation enough. You were right to say that I already know the answers to my questions. My mind seems to be snatching ideas from the ether. If I concentrate, I can chase dozens of possibilities to their logical conclusion."

Phoena's heart overcame her determination to avoid another flashback. Her hand went to the concealed medallion at her throat. Would Baraapa approve of this new champion's talent? That particular nobleman had also seemed without power. He favoured logic over magic. She blinked away other memories and brought her focus back to the room. Yiana's head tilted to the side as she waited for a response.

"What made you suggest the *Academy*?" Phoena asked, trying to keep her expression neutral.

"Lord Westernbrooke's appearance was a big clue," Yiana said. "Did I tell you that I have a brother at the *Academy*? He writes when he needs money." She rubbed her fingers together. "Which means he writes often." Her eyes sparkled with silent laughter. "He said Lord Westernbrooke visited last semester."

Phoena nodded.

"That's not all he said," Yiana continued, waggling a finger. "Senior students were offering a reward for information about a *particular* servant girl. Of course, I wrote back to ask if the maid was attractive. He replied that nobody could remember. Indeed, none of the first years could recall even seeing her. I'd wager that if I brought him here, he'd disavow he knew you, but you could address him by name."

Phoena couldn't stop the corners of her mouth from twitching upwards. She looked directly at Yiana.

"Don't worry," Yiana said with an answering grin. "Your secret is safe with me. I won't even tell Nessie."

Phoena began to protest.

Her new friend shook her head. "It won't be the first secret I've kept from Nessie. As much as I love her, I understand her limitations. She needs to learn how to keep secrets before you tell her the whole story."

CHAPTER 10:
YIANA TAKES CHARGE

Yiana threw her arms around Phoena. "I meant what I said when I accepted the nomination to the Elemental Fellowship. I'm willing to serve you and your quest." She released Phoena and gave her a shove. "Now, go and get changed. You can fix the carpet later."

Phoena went to her dressing room to inspect the flowing green evening gown Nessie had put out for her to wear. It came with a small train. After putting on the dress, she approached the wall-sized mirror. She stared at her reflection, marvelling at her appearance. Cecily was right, she did look like a lady.

Then she came to her senses with a start. Her godmother had said Phoena only needed to stand in front of the mirror and think of her and she would come. Phoena's cheeks reddened at the thought of what Cecily would say about her fussing over her appearance, and she refocused on the dress. There was still so much she didn't understand about these powers.

The neckline was high, but the wide sleeves fell loose from the elbows. With one champion's bangle in plain view, Phoena decided to reveal the other hidden ornaments. She stared at her reflection again. The shiny metal medallion around her neck bore a foreign inscription. What would the Heraldry Master make of that? It was a precious memento.

Baraapa had formed it with his bare hands. The pendant was a reminder that her champions rescued her from the river.

When her hands reached for the dragon brooch pinned to her chest, she closed her eyes. Burning pain in her hand preceded a wave of nostalgia. Abruptly, Phoena turned from her reflection. She must not give in to the temptation to ask the mirror to show her the other champions.

Phoena sighed, crossing the room to the dressing table. She stood before the smaller mirror to fix her hair, still fighting the urge to use the other mirror. Hastily, she caught her hair in a simple knot and rushed to join Yiana.

"Turn around so I can look at you," Yiana said. Phoena obeyed. Yiana pointed at the dragon brooch. "You were wearing that the whole time?" Phoena nodded. "I can't wait to see Fitzgibbon's reaction when he notices it. He wouldn't have challenged you if he'd known you were being courted by the Emberite Ambassador's son."

"I'm not— He's not—"

"Of course *not*," Yiana laughed. "Your red cheeks give you away. One champion gave you this medallion, and the other that bangle. Three potential suitors..."

"When you meet them, you will understand my denial," Phoena said.

Yiana opened her hand to reveal a large, diamond-studded hairpin. It was in the shape of a rolling ocean wave. "Nessie asked me to give you this. Now you have a trinket from each of your elemental champions. Fire, earth, air and water."

"Thank you," Phoena whispered while Yiana fixed it in her dark hair.

Yiana hugged her again. "I only wish that I had something worthy to give you," she said. "My family budget only stretches to semi-precious jewels." She held up her arm, where a multi-coloured strand of gemstones encircled her wrist. The metal clasp was in the shape of a book.

"Can I have a closer look?"

"Of course," Yiana said, unfastening the clasp. "My parents gave it to me for my sixteenth birthday."

Phoena carried it to the fire. She shut her eyes for a moment before throwing the bracelet into the flames. Yiana didn't make a sound. With her eyes still closed, Phoena leaned toward the fireplace. Her power called to the bracelet. Securing her trailing sleeve with the other hand, she thrust her fingers deep into the flames.

Yiana screamed and tried to pull Phoena from the fire. As soon as Yiana touched Phoena, the energy threw the would-be protector backwards. Phoena's scrambling fingers searched for the treasure among the glowing coals.

When Phoena turned from the fire, Yiana lay sprawled on the floor, her back against one of the sofas.

"I'm sorry," Phoena said, hurrying to aid her. "I didn't mean to hurt you."

Yiana grabbed hold of her arm, searching for injury. "You're not burned..."

Phoena opened her hand. There were two strands of gemstones in her palm, identical in every detail. The metal was still glowing from the heat. Phoena waved her other hand, and a shimmering mist settled on the jewels. When the bracelets had cooled, Phoena offered them both to Yiana.

The other girl examined the trinkets. "I don't know which one is the original," Yiana whispered. "But I know enough about gemstones to see that none of these are cheap imitations."

Phoena held out her unadorned arm.

"Oh," Yiana said, fastening one of the strands to Phoena's wrist. "It's probably too big. Your arm is a lot thinner than mine."

Phoena shook her arm, and the new bracelet adjusted itself to the perfect fit. Yiana grinned as she claimed the other bracelet. She tidied her hair before she collected a blue hat from the table beside the door. Then she seized Phoena's hand and propelled her out into the hallway. The pair ran all the way to the dining hall, their laughter filling the stairwell.

When they entered the dining room, they were the first of the seniors to arrive. Yiana strode purposefully to Nessie's chair, and placed the blue hat beside the missing girl's napkin. "We have to reserve her place." She gestured for Phoena to take the seat beside it. When other students arrived, Yiana fielded questions about Nessie's condition. Word of her misadventure had spread to the younger students.

The latest inquirers were departing when the footman announced Meredith's arrival. "This will be interesting," Yiana said. "I've never had to deal with her by myself. Don't let her intimidate you. Just remember that you have more right to sit at Nessie's table than any of the others."

Meredith was distracted by a conversation with her friends. When her eyes registered Phoena's presence, her smile disappeared. She stopped speaking in mid-sentence. Angrily, she turned to Yiana. "You can't sit here. With Nessie in the infirmary, I have seniority. I'm sure there's room for both of you at another table." Her companions echoed their agreement.

"We're not moving," Yiana said with a smile. "You're welcome to join us at *our* table, or if you don't care for our company, *you* can take yourself elsewhere."

Meredith frowned at the hat. "Why did you bring *that* to the table?" she asked in a loud voice. One of her allies reached for the offending item.

"I wouldn't," Yiana said in a commanding voice. "There's no telling what magical protections are in that hat." The girl pulled her hand back in alarm. More than one gasp filled the silence. Yiana grinned.

She filled Phoena's water glass while acting as if Meredith and her friends had left. Phoena peered over the top of her tumbler as Meredith consulted her companions. Three of them walked away, relegated to another table. The others claimed their seats as if they were eager not to miss any further revelations. Meredith sat opposite Nessie's hat. One of her friends sat beside it.

An uncomfortable silence drifted outwards to the nearby tables. All eyes seemed to focus on their group.

Yiana took advantage of the moment. "The nurse said Nessie's lucky to survive her latest attempt at magic."

"Is it true that she's turned blue?" one of the girls asked.

"Shh!" said another. "Mrs Hammersley has just arrived."

Every girl in the room leapt to their feet as their teachers entered in single file. When the adults were seated at the head table, Mrs Hammersley surveyed the dining room. Her eye lingered on Nessie's empty chair before she took her seat. At this signal, everyone else copied her action.

The servants carried steaming bowls of vegetable soup into the dining room. Phoena was surprised with the small portion size – she consumed every mouthful without being too full. The second course quickly followed. The fish fillet sat beside a dainty garden salad. She devoured it hungrily and discovered that she still had an appetite for more. As she waited for the third course – the menu said roast lamb – her mind drifted to the *Westernbrooke Academy* dining hall. The young noblemen there dined from larger plates that were piled high.

Phoena closed her eyes. She remembered what it was like to always be hungry. The *Academy* kitchens prepared mountains of rich food, but Phoena had dined frugally – and only when her work was complete. Often, she had been too exhausted to eat. She sighed. Hopefully, the kitchen staff here found it easier to keep these girls fed.

As the maids began clearing the plates, there was a commotion at the main entrance. Everyone froze, and the headmistress rose to her feet. A footman came towards the head table and whispered to Mrs Hammersley. She frowned and sent him back to the door.

"What was that about?" Meredith asked her neighbour, turning in her chair to watch the footman. He seized the handle and wrenched the door open.

A flurry of blue ruffles and lace launched herself into the room. Nessie ran to the headmistress, pulling up at the last minute. "Sorry, Headmistress," she panted, smoothing her blue skirts and adjusting her hairstyle. "You put a spell on the room, and it took me longer to escape than I expected."

Mrs Hammersley's reply was too low to hear. Nessie dashed to her table and threw herself into her seat. "So that's where my hat disappeared to," she cried, thrusting it to one side. A servant placed a plate of food before her. The maid was staring at Nessie's blue hair, made more conspicuous because she had added a massive feather. Phoena's eyes were still fixed on the maid when Meredith shrieked.

"I'm sure you did that on purpose," Meredith hissed, leaping to her feet. Water streamed across the table from the spilled carafe. "It happens too often to be excused by your clumsiness."

"Stop making a fuss," Nessie said, righting the carafe. As she moved her hand, the water reversed itself and returned to the crystal vessel. Everyone froze.

"H-how—" Meredith spluttered.

"That was easy," Nessie laughed, "compared to the trouble I had removing the blue potion from my skin. The headmistress put a spell on the door so that I could only leave when the blue was gone."

"But your hair—" another girl began.

"She didn't think to include my hair." Nessie turned her head this way and that. The unbound tresses shimmered in the candlelight. "Lovely, isn't it?" she said. "I've decided to keep it this way, as a reminder that I'm not an easy target anymore." She flashed a smile around the table. "Anyone want some water?" she asked, the carafe in her hand.

Meredith declined the offer. Instead, she signalled a servant to refill her wine glass. The maid topped up the other wine glasses before retreating. Nessie said, "Water's not the only liquid I can play with." She laughed, and the wine in Meredith's glass began to dance.

Meredith hastily put down her drink, and the colour drained from her face. "What's happened to you?"

"Sworn to secrecy," Nessie said, winking at Meredith.

Phoena shot Yiana a startled look after her friend kicked her under the table. "You're allowed to laugh now," Yiana said and set an excellent example.

Meredith and her friends abandoned the dining room as soon as permissible. Well-wishers swarmed around Nessie, eager to touch her hair. Nessie sighed, declaring this the most enjoyable experience ever. They were still seated at the table when a footman announced that Phoena's coach was waiting to take her home.

CHAPTER II:
NESSIE'S SURPRISE

The days flew past. The first week of the semester was nearly over. Phoena arrived on Friday without the familiar fear of rejection. She was learning to trust Yiana, who always guided her through difficult situations. Dancing was the first lesson for today, which gave her little concern. Phoena was grateful that Ennallya and Cecily had taught her the basic dance moves. All she had to do was remember to smile and try not to step on her partner's toes.

The second lesson was still-life painting. It should have been a pleasant experience, but Phoena's peace abandoned her. She searched for the origins of her apprehension. As the clock counted down to midday, Phoena's fingers tingled with restless power. What was happening? Any stronger, and fiery blue sparks would be on display.

She glanced at her companions. Yiana frowned at Nessie, who was staring out the window, twirling her paintbrush. Did the prickly pain in Phoena's hands have something to do with the blue-haired girl's daydreaming? Nessie had shown remarkable restraint since the unveiling of her hair.

Publicly, she had only exercised her new powers while teasing Meredith at mealtimes. As Nessie's notoriety increased, Meredith's temper soured. Yesterday, the cousins had provoked each other at every opportunity. Mrs Hammersley had taken them aside for an official warning. Today, the cousins were ignoring each other.

The lesson ended. Nessie broke from her reverie with a cry of delight, leaping to her feet. "Come on!" She pulled the others along as she hurried into the hall. Phoena glanced towards Meredith, who whispered with her friends.

"What's the rush?" Yiana asked.

"Wait and see," Nessie said, leading them up the stairs. She shouldered her way through the other students. "I've planned a surprise for this afternoon."

Yiana groaned. "I don't want any trouble."

"It's not that kind of surprise," Nessie protested, but then she missed the next step. Yiana grabbed her before she fell. "At least, I hope it's not." Nessie kept her thoughts to herself for the remainder of the climb.

"Tell me now," Yiana said when they were safely on the third-floor landing. "I don't like it when you're quiet. I'm not in the mood for a mystery."

"Oh, all right," Nessie said. "It's nothing to worry about. I have visitors coming for the afternoon. I've reserved the Rose Drawing Room and ordered high tea."

"That's the surprise?" Yiana sounded sceptical.

"Mama sent me a message this morning," Nessie said, pushing open Phoena's door. She led them inside as if she owned the suite. "You know Mama's throwing a ball tomorrow. She's sending a delegation to confirm that my blueness won't prevent my attendance."

Entering the dressing room, Nessie opened Phoena's wardrobe. Nessie pulled out a grey dress and held it in front of Phoena. "I'm sure my mother has at least two potential suitors lined up. She's suspicious that I've turned blue to thwart her plans."

"Who's coming this afternoon?" Yiana asked.

Nessie grinned and dropped into a low curtsey.

"Not the Princess Royal?" Yiana cried. "She never goes anywhere without a crowd."

"That's why I've reserved the Rose Drawing Room," Nessie said. She selected another dress and dismissed it immediately. "Phoena, don't you have anything that isn't in earthy tones?"

Nessie tossed the dress to Yiana to rehang. "Princess Ivandelle's bound to have a few eligible bachelors with her. We couldn't *possibly* bring them up here to the third floor. All the other girls would expect an invitation, and I want to keep Phoena's suite for ourselves. Meredith is going to be green with envy when she finds out I didn't include her."

"I don't think it's wise to keep needling your cousin," Yiana said. "It's not easy for her, living in your shadow. She had every reason to expect you to be married before now. She thought she would be queen bee this year."

"If I annoy her enough, perhaps she'll get married first, just to spite me."

"She's only fifteen."

Nessie pulled a face. "Both her mother and mine were married at fifteen." She shook her head. "I wish you had something brighter, Phoena. I want you to make a good impression." She tossed a brown dress with white lace trim towards the divan. "This will have to do. If you weren't so tall, I'd lend you one of my dresses."

Phoena retrieved the garment from the floor.

Nessie resumed her argument. "If you listen to our relatives, Meredith and I are in danger of becoming old maids." She admired herself in the larger mirror before turning to Yiana. "Your mother must be worried about you, too. In two months, you'll be eighteen."

"No one expects me to marry," Yiana said. "There's no dowry. If I hadn't won a scholarship, I'd already be working. At least with an education I can be someone's governess or an academic's personal assistant, instead of working in a shop."

"We can't have that," Nessie said. "There's plenty of widowers who would settle for someone without money–"

Yiana flinched. "I'm going to change," she said, hurrying from the room.

Nessie chased Yiana from the room. "Don't be cross with me. I'll ask my cousin Karil if he has any suggestions..."

Phoena waited until she heard the hallway door open and close. She walked to the mystical mirror and took a deep breath. "Cecily, I need answers." The mirror clouded. When the mist cleared, it revealed her godmother's reassuring presence. "I'm so glad you're there." Phoena began without preamble. "I'm about to meet the Princess Royal."

"I know."

"You do?"

"She arrived unannounced this morning." Cecily's small smile was not reassuring.

"What did she want?"

"Nessie's mother is hosting a ball tomorrow," Cecily said, "and our invitation seems to have been mislaid. Ivandelle came to Sumnarscote to ensure our attendance."

"You said 'we'? Surely I don't have to go?"

"But of course you do. That's one of the reasons we enrolled you at *Quenthlaretta College*. It's important for you to be *seen*. However, we didn't expect you to recruit Fellowship candidates the moment you arrived."

"Is the Princess Royal a member of the Fellowship?"

Cecily stiffened. "Most certainly not! Under no circumstances are you to trust anything that woman says. She was a self-serving schemer when we were at school. Nothing I've heard recently suggests anything has changed."

"Nessie admires her," Phoena said. "I'm sure she will tell the Princess Royal everything."

"Then you and Yiana will have to ensure Nessie doesn't have an opportunity."

CHAPTER 12:
ENTERTAINING ROYALTY

Phoena and Yiana slipped into the private pantry through the servants' entrance. Two maids looked up from preparing the refreshments. Phoena smiled. She recognised them both from the blue-carpet incident in her suite. She put her finger to her lips and brought out her purse. Both maids relaxed. They each pocketed a silver coin before resuming their work. Yiana went to the other door and cracked it open. Nessie's voice was easy to hear – she was delivering the rehearsed fictional account of her transformation.

The two friends peered through the narrow gap into the Rose Drawing Room. The floral curtains and wallpaper would have overpowered a smaller room. There were rose-filled vases on the tables between the windows. The garden view was lovely, but the distant river was hidden behind a hedge.

The Princess Royal and her guests were seated on sofas arranged around a low table. Phoena scanned the group. Yiana pointed to the Princess, who sat by herself. Phoena nodded. She had already guessed her identity. There was a dark cloud of sizzling energy around Princess Ivandelle. Pulsating strands of purple mist flowed outward as if they were seeking something.

The dark plum colour intensified for a few moments and then seemed to withdraw. Phoena almost relaxed, and then the Princess looked directly at the pantry door.

Phoena's power flared in response. With a yelp, Yiana pulled her back from the door. Their hair stood out from their heads, and blue light flickered around them. Then both girls began rising above the floor. There was a sudden brilliant flash, and growling thunder shook the pantry.

Yiana gasped. When she released Phoena, Yiana fell to the floor. The shaking girl leaned against the door, her face pale. Phoena drifted down a few seconds later. She glanced over at the maids, who were pretending not to have noticed anything.

"Can you see her magic?" Phoena whispered.

"I couldn't at first," Yiana said, "but then you zapped me. I've never seen anything like the aura around Princess Ivandelle. Is it safe for you to go in there?"

"I don't have a choice. She already knows there's a powerful presence here. If I run away, she'll think I'm a threat."

Yiana dropped her voice even lower. "Are you?"

"Shh," Phoena said. "I need to see who else is here."

The Princess Royal returned her attention to Nessie's story. A strand of purple mist hovered in a spiral over the storyteller.

The Princess sat tall, proud and alert. She wore an extravagant hat and a colourful costume that accentuated her curves. Upon the next sofa perched three women who seemed no older than Nessie. They were smiling at Nessie's excitement.

There was a sameness about them, both in mannerisms and dress. When Phoena concentrated, she could see purple bands of darkness at their wrists.

The Princess's four male companions were more varied. A grey-bearded man with a haughty demeanour sat on another sofa, adjacent to Nessie. He wore a long robe similar to the ones preferred by Lord Westernbrooke, Phoena's godfather. The man beside him was younger, perhaps in his early thirties. There was a strong family resemblance. Father and son?

The younger man had dark hair, worn loose down to his broad shoulders. His trimmed beard was short, emphasising his proud countenance. He wore a black ruffled jacket and waist-length cape, similar in style to the *Academy* masters. His tight leather trousers were tucked into knee-length boots.

The other two men were seated with their backs to the door. One of them was wearing an elaborately decorated cape and a gold band around his head. The final man was taller, with a muscular physique. He wore his wavy hair long, and there was something in the way he sat that reminded her of Karilion.

She hastily pushed away that thought. "I've seen enough."

Phoena turned to the maids and inspected their trolley. She slipped them each another coin, waiting for Cecily's loyalty charm to activate. Phoena knew how easily gossip spread, and she wanted to be doubly sure these servants kept any hint that she had magical powers a secret.

They each dropped into a low curtsey. "Thank you, Miss."

Satisfied, Phoena went to the fire. She swung the kettle away from the flames. With exaggerated care, she poured boiling water over the tea leaves. There were two different blends of tea, served from distinctive rose-patterned teapots. Phoena savoured the fragrant steam for a moment before placing the lid on each teapot. After she stepped away, the maids wheeled the trolley into the drawing-room.

Nessie was concluding her story. "And there you have it. That's how I got my blue hair." She sprang to her feet when she saw Yiana and Phoena enter behind the trolley. "And here are my witnesses – Yiana, you can confirm my tale. I'm sure some of my guests don't believe me." A ripple of laughter followed Nessie's remark. "Princess Ivandelle, of course you remember my friend, Lady Yiana Yianothalis?"

Yiana bobbed politely. The Princess smiled at Yiana. The purple mist drifted from around Nessie towards the plump girl before withdrawing. The Princess waved Yiana to the empty sofa immediately beside her.

Princess Ivandelle leaned forward, her attention fixed on Phoena. The purple mist held back as if uncertain how to proceed. Every nerve in Phoena's body tingled. She could feel the blue sparks waiting to fly from her fingers at the slightest provocation.

Of greater concern were the dark swirling shadows growing beneath her feet. Phoena offered up a prayer that her powerful defences would behave. She knew that only she could see this phenomenon. The consequences, should she disappear in front of these influential witnesses, were unthinkable. It would be impossible to preserve her anonymity.

"Miss Feeee-nahhh Ashh-ton." Nessie stretched out the syllables. "Goddaughter to Lady Cecily de Montnoir."

Phoena curtsied. There was an awkward silence. Carefully she raised her eyes and saw that Princess Ivandelle was studying her. The Princess must have motioned for Nessie to be seated because Phoena stood alone.

"Fee-nahh is an unusual name," Princess Ivandelle said, and her purple mist pulsed and quivered.

A small twitch above her Highness's right eyebrow was the only sign that her sneaky mind-reading spell had failed. *Had the royal visitor hoped to gain an advantage by using Phoena's true name?* The Princess leaned back against the upholstery. "I'm not familiar with your history. Who were your parents? Where have you come from?"

Phoena considered her answer. The only sound came from the maids as they unloaded the trolley. She watched them from the corner of her eye. When she was sure that they had returned to the pantry, she spoke.

"I can offer no satisfactory answer to either question, Highness," Phoena said. "I'm a foundling."

The female courtiers gasped, Princess Ivandelle frowned, the purple mist darkened.

Phoena pretended not to notice, directing their attention towards the refreshments. "The teapot with the red rose pattern has a more delicate blend. It should be perfectly brewed now. I will tell you what I can of my story while you enjoy your tea."

"You can pour," Princess Ivandelle said. An indignant huff arose from the other ladies. This must be a sought-after honour. The Princess silenced them with a glance. "But first, I must introduce you to my entourage. My ladies-in-waiting are too eager today, so I had better mention them first. Lady Avarina, her younger sister, Lady Hillarina, and Lady Cassandee." The women nodded to acknowledge their names, smiling sweetly at their Princess.

Phoena curtsied to each one before swivelling towards the remaining nobility.

Princess Ivandelle waved her hand towards the elder gentleman. "Duke Urdigo of Umbryden, and his son Xavier, Marquis of Umbryden." Both men studied Phoena as if she were a prize exhibit, and it was a relief that the Princess moved on quickly.

"Prince Braevin, our cousin; third in line to the throne." This prince was the one wearing a thin circlet of gold around his head. He had a long narrow face and a bored look about him.

"And our youngest companion, Lord Karilion of Hemington. We call him Karil, and he can always be relied upon for amusement."

Phoena gave the last nobleman no more than a passing glance. But inside, she struggled to maintain her composure. What was one of her champions doing here? And did the Princess know she was already acquainted with the eighteen-year-old nobleman?

A sly glance passed between the Princess and her cousin, Prince Braevin. A strand of purple shadow raced across the room at the Princess's direction. It spun around Karilion and then became a thin band on his wrist. Karilion leapt to his feet before Phoena could catch her breath.

Was Karilion under the Princess's control? Phoena battled the gathering darkness as her heart raced. She had to know if he would betray her. That would reveal how dangerous the Princess Royal could be.

The moment stretched as he approached. Phoena remembered the occasion when Karilion had tried to use a coercive enchantment on her at the *Academy*. But the other student magic-users present had protested. Their outrage had proved that his controlling spell was easily detectable. This purple mist must be different. Nobody reacted, not even Karilion, who did not deflect it.

Before Phoena could defend herself, Karilion rounded the table. Yiana and Nessie cried out in alarm. The Princess commanded the young women to remain seated. The enchanted nobleman lifted Phoena from the floor, spinning her with him in a crazy dance.

"Forgive my boldness, My Lady," he laughed, "for I must play the fool."

When Karilion came to a stop, Phoena still faced the Princess, but his broad frame was like a living shield. He brought his face close to her, and his long hair became a veil. She gasped. "Shh!" he whispered and attempted to kiss her.

What kind of game was he playing? Phoena's right hand instinctively flew up to slap him. Karilion caught Phoena's wrist before she could strike. He folded her fingers and lightly kissed them. "We'll talk later," he breathed.

In a louder voice, he said, "Miss Ashton, your beauty has cast a spell on me. I don't care where you were found. I'm only glad to have you here in my arms." He stepped back, making a show of admiring her curves. Phoena felt the colour rise in her cheeks. "Please don't ever lose yourself again."

Then he turned towards the couch. "Move over," he said to Nessie. "I'm going to sit here with my true love." He sat, pulling Phoena down close beside him.

Nessie and Yiana both reached for Phoena, their voices loud in protest.

"Children," Princess Ivandelle said. "Relax and enjoy the fun. The spell will be exhausted in a few minutes, and then Karil will be mortified by his behaviour."

Karilion continued to grin at Phoena as if she was his prize.

"What spell?" Nessie asked, a worried expression on her face.

"Our best magicians and apothecaries have been unable to explain this," Prince Braevin said.

Phoena carefully controlled her face. She nudged Yiana, who was ready to disavow his claim. The Princess must remain unaware that both of them could see the magic purple band on Karilion's arm. Phoena crept her hand closer to the secret spell, ready to release him with her power.

"This has happened to Karil once or twice," the Princess said. "There's no telling when the next attack will occur, but this is the first time he has chosen an unwilling maiden. As you can see, he's a determined flirt, but I assure you that your friend will escape from his arms with her honour intact."

The Princess's entourage found this situation amusing. Phoena turned her head to hide her anger. The tingling in her fingers intensified. If Karilion didn't come to his senses soon, there would be no hiding her supernatural reaction.

Karilion pretended to nibble her ear. "Don't let her win," he whispered. He stroked her hair and held her tight. "Trust me." Phoena took a deep breath and endured his embrace.

"Nessie," Princess Ivandelle said, "this is why I've warned you to keep magical protections about you. Imagine the consequences if you threw yourself at someone like this." The other ladies from her entourage giggled. "My apothecaries have created a preventative remedy."

Karilion stiffened. Phoena peeked to see what was offered to her friend. Princess Ivandelle held a glowing purple bangle. Nessie reached out her hand.

"What's that?" Yiana asked warily. She glanced at the other three ladies, who each held up their arms. They wore identical bangles.

"A little trinket to keep Nessie safe," Princess Ivandelle said. "I'm sorry that I didn't bring another one, or I could have offered you protection, too."

"I'd rather take my chances," Yiana muttered.

Nessie examined the bangle eagerly. The grinning girl flashed with blue energy to match her growing excitement. Phoena had seen that look before and dreaded what was to come. Yiana placed her hand on Phoena's shoulder, alarm in her eyes. The last time Nessie had lost control of her emotions like this, she had dumped blue dye over herself.

Karilion's muscles tensed, and the arm that held Phoena tightened. She could feel his awakening power with every molecule of her being. Her heart skipped like a mountain goat, and the room began to spin.

Everything happened at once.

Nessie pounced on Karilion. "He needs it more than I do," she cried as she rammed the new bangle down over the wrist that already wore the magic band.

"No!" cried Yiana, throwing herself at Nessie.

"Stop!" shouted the Princess.

"Sunlight!" cried Karilion and squeezed Phoena tight. That single word unlocked something deep within her. A blinding light, brighter than the noonday sun, drove all thought from her mind.

Ka-BOOM!

CHAPTER 13:
TAUNTS AND ACCUSATIONS

Phoena sat with her eyes closed, assessing her situation. Coloured flashes, leftover from the explosion, flickered on the inside of her eyelids. Her mind protested about going somewhere without permission. Meanwhile, her body catalogued her pain.

After a few moments, she confirmed that there was no serious injury from the explosion.

Karilion shifted beside her, his arm still around her waist. "This is an improvement."

If not for the sound of running water – and the warm breeze blowing across her face – she might convince herself that they were still in the drawing-room. Phoena did not want to find herself underground again. That was how her last adventure began.

"Where's Nessie?" Yiana's voice sounded too loud.

Phoena cracked open her eyes, fearing what she might discover. Yiana lay on a grassy riverbank near slow-moving water. She seemed shaken but otherwise unharmed.

"Where else?" Karilion said, pointing with his arm.

A short distance away, Nessie was waist-deep in the river. She struggled towards the shallows. "You could come to help me," Nessie cried as she pulled herself onto the riverbank. She wasn't smiling. Her water-logged dress made it difficult to walk. "Would someone *please* explain how *I* ended up in the river, while *Karil* remains dry on that sofa?"

Phoena was shocked. Only now did she realise the piece of furniture had travelled with them.

"Don't be angry with me," Karilion chortled. "I did what I could to ensure we stayed out in the sunshine. You'd have more reason to complain if you'd landed in a subterranean river."

Nessie grumbled as she sloshed towards them. It would take her some time to cross the distance in her full skirts. Phoena pushed at Karilion's arm. He released her with a cheeky grin, and she stepped out of his reach. He held up his arm to show her that the menacing spell was no longer on his wrist.

"Is that why you shouted 'sunlight'?" Phoena asked. "To make sure we stayed above ground."

"You've done this before?" Yiana asked, standing closer. "I've never heard of a single-word spell. I'm surprised a show-off like you could keep that to yourself."

"Who are you calling a show-off?" He pulled a face at Yiana, and then he grinned. "As much as I'd like to take the credit, it wasn't *me*."

"Well, it certainly wasn't me," complained Nessie as she rejoined them. "All I can do is play with water." To illustrate her point, she began shaking herself like a wet puppy. Instead of water spraying in every direction, a directed stream targeted her cousin.

"Hey!" Karilion cried, raising his arms in defence. "My Lady, make her behave."

Phoena lifted her hand, and the spurt of water disappeared. Nessie's clothes and hair were suddenly dry. Nessie's mouth opened wide. Karilion tilted his chin towards

Phoena. "I'm one of her *favourites*," he said smugly, "so you have to be nice to me."

Nessie rushed at him. "You!" she shouted. He dragged Phoena in front of him as a shield.

"Are you saying that *Phoena* is responsible for this?" Yiana asked.

"I'm not sure how she does it," Karilion said. "But whenever Phoena disappears, anyone touching her gets dragged along too. We've been trying different methods to influence the destination. 'Sunlight' worked better than I expected!"

"Why would you want to influence her?"

"Oramis thinks her magic is too protective." Karilion shrugged. "If it decides someone is a threat to Phoena, it sends them somewhere else."

Nessie began to flap her arms, her face red. "Are you implying I'm—"

He ignored her. "The first time it happened to me, I was lost underground for hours before I found anyone else. Baraapa had it far worse than Oramis or I because he couldn't magic himself any light."

"So if we're touching Phoena, she can transport all of us," Yiana said. "I think I can see how we came to be here. I seized the back of the sofa to keep my balance, but I must have been touching Phoena when I grabbed Nessie's wrist. It felt like the sofa was flying through the air, but I thought that was because of the explosion."

"So how did I end up in the water?" Nessie asked.

"You were holding that magic bracelet," Yiana replied. "I realised too late that you couldn't see the magic band glowing on his wrist. You didn't know that Karil was already under the influence of some kind of spell. Sparks flew in all directions as the gap between both spells decreased. I'm guessing the two spells combined to make the explosion. Perhaps the force threw you away from us."

"Or perhaps Phoena's magic thinks you have divided allegiances," Karilion said. He was serious now. "You've always been easily influenced by the Princess."

"You can talk," Nessie said. "You were playing her jester."

"I have my orders," he said. "The Fellowship needs information about these spells, which are causing embarrassment at Court."

"You're just making excuses," Nessie said, "because the magic spell was too strong for you to deflect it."

"I could have disabled it in a moment," Karilion cried. "Just like that." He clicked his fingers. "I never let them coerce me into doing anything that I wouldn't do if the *right* opportunity presented itself. I want the Princess Royal to keep me close."

"Are you suggesting that Princess Ivandelle has something to do with these spells?" Nessie demanded.

"We can talk about this later," Yiana said. "What we have to decide now is whether we go back. I'm surprised they haven't already discovered us here. We're still on College grounds."

"Is that where we are?" Phoena asked, for the first time looking further than her immediate surroundings. Landscaped gardens and manicured lawn separated them from the College buildings.

"There's something of greater urgency," Karilion said. "We have to come up with an explanation that doesn't reveal Phoena's secrets."

CHAPTER 14: A DARK VISITATION

Phoena's three companions energetically debated their situation. Nessie and Karilion spoke over the top of each other, with Yiana adding her opinion when either of them paused to breathe. No-one questioned Phoena's silence. Perhaps they didn't think she had anything to contribute to the discussion? She pushed aside her wounded pride. This new emotion made it difficult to focus. Her heart and mind battled over what took precedence: loyalty to her friends or self-preservation? Her power surged, demanding action. If only it would tell her whether she should fight or flee.

After a heated discussion, the other two champions agreed with Yiana's simple plan. They would pretend they didn't know what caused their disappearance. The first step was to return the missing furniture to the Rose Drawing Room. Karilion approached the large sofa and hoisted it in the air. It wobbled precariously, and he staggered. He adjusted his grip and then dropped it.

Next, he walked to the carved armrest. "Girls, pick up the other end." He removed his jacket and tossed it onto the sofa.

Flexing his muscles, he lifted his end from the ground. "It's only a short distance. I'd carry it myself if it weren't a three-seater. I only need you to stop your end from dragging on the ground."

Without hesitation, Phoena stepped forward to test the weight.

"Phoena can do it by herself," Nessie said. "She's stronger than she looks."

"I'm okay with the weight," Phoena said with an easy smile. Karilion raised an eyebrow. Perhaps he didn't know that members of the Fellowship were continuing her training? The regular physical exercise had built on the strength her servitude had developed.

Karilion shrugged. He turned his back and adjusted his grip, his white shirt stretched taut across his muscular shoulders. Phoena followed him with ease, but she allowed him to set the pace.

"Wait, Karil," Yiana said.

He put down the sofa. His hands went to his hips.

"Nessie, we have to help." Yiana grabbed the back of the sofa. "We can't leave Phoena to carry this load without us. She's not our servant." Her chubby face contorted as she searched for a better handhold. "And stop telling people that Phoena is more than she appears. That will only bring more trouble."

"Karil already knows about Phoena," Nessie grumbled, taking up the lower side. She had an easier task than Yiana. "I'm careful who I tell."

Karilion laughed as he resumed the lead position. "You, Nessie? Careful? Everything you do is to attract attention to yourself."

"What!" Nessie cried, her feet shuffling to keep up with his long strides. "Next thing I know, you'll be blaming me for this mess. If you hadn't been playing the fool, none of this would have happened."

"And if you hadn't been so keen to show off—"

"Stop it, both of you," Yiana said. "I'm tired of this petty sniping. The sooner we return this sofa and go our separate ways, the better."

Nessie pouted. Phoena adjusted her hands and enjoyed the brief reprieve from their disagreement. She settled into a comfortable rhythm. Karilion made slower progress than she expected. She looked across the lawns towards the College entrance. By the time they were a third of the way to their destination, Phoena's mind had drifted.

It was a warm afternoon, a pleasant day for a garden stroll. The peaceful burble of the river faded. Phoena had to concentrate to hear it above the droning insects and the quiet whirring of wings. Those creatures were flying to and fro, revelling in their freedom. She surveyed the scene. Not a gardener in sight. How delightful it would be if she could tell her companions to leave her here.

She glanced forward. Karilion refused to admit that the wooden-framed sofa was heavier than he expected. His steps were less certain. As she watched, he half-stumbled over the root of a tree. They were taking another "short-cut" between meandering walkways.

He jostled the weight. "It will be easier when we get to the next path."

"You've said that before," Nessie muttered, her face red. "You keep promising it will get easier. Well, it isn't." The blue-haired girl seemed on the verge of tears. "Why can't we stop?"

Phoena's heart jumped within her chest. What use was her power if she could not use it to help her friends? In answer, a small burst of energy flowed through her hands.

The sofa raised itself a little higher above the ground. Yiana glanced at Phoena and smiled. "Thank you," she mouthed. "Just be careful."

Nessie gave no sign that she noticed the lighter load, but Karilion stood straighter. Instead of allowing everyone some respite, he lengthened his stride. Nessie's complaints intensified, making it more difficult for Phoena to concentrate. Ignoring her friend's whining should have been easy.

But then Karilion began responding with snippy remarks. This nastiness between the cousins was harder to overlook. Phoena's irritation at her lack of self-discipline increased.

Something's wrong. She searched for a reason for her increased apprehension. A brooding heaviness drew nearer. The sky was clear, yet a dark shadow hovered over their group. When an oppressive weariness pressed upon her shoulders, Phoena bowed under the weight. The going was more difficult than before.

Was she tiring, or was this sensation caused by something else? A prickliness ran across her back and down her arms. This sensation confirmed her suspicion that someone had discovered them. She pushed down a sudden compulsion to demonstrate her power – to declare to the world that she was not to be trifled with. Karilion's earlier criticism about Nessie showing off was a cautionary reminder. Her Fellowship teachers kept insisting that Phoena was here for a longer game.

How did the searchers find them? Usually, nobody could detect the presence of her kind of power. That didn't seem to apply to the Princess's purple mist. Then Phoena stared at her friends. Karilion and Nessie bristled with magical energy, acting like beacons.

Phoena glanced towards Yiana. Her intuitive friend searched the sky.

A harsh cry rang out. Phoena almost dropped the sofa in alarm. Her eyes hunted for the source. *There!* A large black bird came swooping across the garden towards them. For a moment, the whole world fell silent. The pounding of her heart matched the *swhoosh-whoosh-swhoosh* from the approaching bird.

The huge raven circled twice before settling in a tree branch just ahead of them. It cocked its head to one side as if it studied them. Nessie and Karilion didn't pause in their disagreement. Couldn't they sense the raven's ominous presence?

Yiana coughed. The muscles in Phoena's back twitched at the sound. Her concern moved to Yiana, who hunched over the sofa. Yiana's knuckles were white as if she was in danger of dropping her burden. The temptation to use more of her power intensified. Phoena struggled to maintain control of her emotions. Which of the many options was the best one?

Karilion stopped suddenly. "I need another rest," he said, thumping the furniture to the ground.

Phoena's mind screamed, *Another rest?* The physical jolt from his abrupt action sent ripples of pain through her back and shoulders. An involuntary cry escaped her mouth. Spiteful thoughts flooded her mind. She swallowed the bitterness of nasty criticism souring her stomach. What kind of dark sorcery had the bird delivered? She chewed her lip, wrapping her arms around her chest as she stepped away. It helped if she wasn't looking at the group.

"You selfish idiot," Yiana snapped, and Phoena cringed at the poison in her tone. "You could have given us some warning. That hurt."

"I don't know why you're complaining," Karilion said. "You girls are useless. It feels as if I'm carrying this sofa by myself."

"Useless!" Nessie cried, her voice rising to a screech. "You're the one who boasted that you didn't *need* our help."

Yiana appeared beside Phoena. "Are you okay?" she whispered. Phoena nodded. She studied her friend for signs of anger, but there was only a troubled smile. Yiana put her arm around Phoena. She turned them both toward the others. The raven was closer now, perched in a branch above Karilion's head.

"I've been asking you to stop for the past five minutes," Nessie went on. She stomped towards Karilion, her blue hair sizzling. He stood glaring down his nose at the shorter teenager, his arms folded across his broad chest. She shoved him, and he fell backwards. "Carrying the sofa was *your* stupid idea."

"I didn't hear you suggest anything better," Karilion said, scrambling to his feet. The angry pair faced each other.

"You could have magicked it back," Nessie said.

"You never listen! I told you I didn't magic the sofa!"

"Well, none of us did," Nessie retorted. "It must have been you. You're the one who's always popping in and out, making mischief."

"That was when I was a kid," Karilion said. "And you know I can only move myself into the next room." He took a deep breath. "Do you think I'd be standing here with *you* and your little friends if I could magic myself back?"

"You would if you had another motive," Nessie sneered. "You're still trying to impress Phoena."

"Why would I want to impress a nobody like her? I wouldn't have looked twice at her if it hadn't been for that blasted spell."

"You're only saying that because she reje–"

"That's enough!" Yiana said, stepping between them. "This isn't getting the sofa any closer to the building."

"I'm not carrying it any further," Nessie said. "I'm going to walk back and find some footmen. They can help him carry it." She glared at Yiana. "Are you coming with me, or have you fallen under Karil's spell?" Without waiting, Nessie lifted her skirts to her knees and ran.

"I am *not* under Karil's spell!" Yiana protested. "Come on, Phoena." She dragged Phoena after Nessie. Phoena cast a glance over her shoulder. Karilion stood under the tree, watching them leave.

The menacing bird took flight. Its beating wings came so near to the departing girls the momentum ruffled Phoena's hair. Both girls ducked, clinging to each other.

The raven cawed as it soared towards the College. The noise sounded like evil laughter. Within minutes, the bird disappeared from view behind the building. Neither girl spoke.

Despite her earlier protests, Nessie showed no sign of exhaustion. She was almost to the main driveway now. The Princess Royal's coach, and one other, had prime position in the College forecourt. As Yiana and Phoena endeavoured to catch up with Nessie, two figures came around the coaches. Although the distance was great, Phoena could guess their identity.

Nessie ran to greet them. From the energetic way she waved her arms, she was telling her tale to two of the Princess Royal's companions. One of them put his arm around Nessie's shoulder to escort her across the forecourt. The two men ushered their friend up the stone steps, and she disappeared indoors.

"Come on," Yiana panted. "Nessie's likely to tell them too much."

CHAPTER 15:
A DANGEROUS INTERVIEW

Phoena was once more in the Rose Drawing Room. The three girls sat on a mismatched sofa, brought in to imitate the original arrangement. It clashed with the design of the wallpaper. Perhaps that contributed to the strange tension in the room? Phoena perched awkwardly between her two friends, poised for flight. Yiana placed a restraining hand on her elbow.

The courtiers were seated as before.

Except for Karilion. The young nobleman had stormed in a few minutes ago, footmen following at his heels with the sofa. The Princess had waved dismissively and the servants withdrew with the offending furniture.

Laughter and jibes from the other adults had greeted Karilion's return. Princess Ivandelle didn't join in with the ridicule, but she did nothing to dissuade them. Nessie contributed to his discomfort by adding some nasty taunts. The youth had retreated to the hearth, where he sulked.

Only the Princess directly faced the fire burning in the fireplace. The radiating heat strengthened Phoena's resolve. Taking a deep breath, she assessed the atmosphere in the room. The Princess was her main concern, but Nessie's mood was growing more dangerous.

The oppressive darkness from the garden was gone. Phoena was confident that they were free of that controlling influence. Yet their unpredictable friend's anger hadn't faded. The blue-haired girl sat closest to the Princess. Her back rested against the cushions, but her crossed leg jerked in a violent rhythm.

Nessie's eyes locked on Karilion. Her tapping fingertips threatened more trouble. "One day, someone is going to unmask you as a bully and a coward."

The watching Princess leaned forward with a frown. "Nessie," she said. Her icy tone was a clear warning. "That is no way to speak to your dear cousin. He's only just turned eighteen, so he cannot help his youthful foolishness."

Nessie sneered. "He has seriously offended me – and my friends."

Phoena almost leapt to her feet. Yiana increased the pressure on her arm.

"Lord Karilion, come here," Princess Ivandelle commanded. The nobleman hesitated for a moment. The Princess raised her chin and sat taller on her seat. In response, he straightened his posture. Then he approached from the other side of the low table. "Karil, apologise to Nessie."

He turned stiffly. "Nessie, I apologise for offending you – and your friends." He followed his words with a stiff bow. Nessie remained seated, responding with the briefest nod.

"Your sullen behaviour is unbecoming," the Princess said to Nessie. "It's your turn to apologise."

"And if I refuse?" Nessie demanded.

The mist around the Princess darkened. Could Her Highness see the sparks of blue energy that flashed around

Nessie? Phoena's skin tingled. The Princess's countenance didn't alter, but Karilion's eyes widened in alarm. She saw him summon his defences in readiness. Something hovered in the air above him, but he didn't launch an attack towards his cousin. Instead, his arm reached across the table towards Nessie's hand. The angry girl slapped it away. The air hissed as their respective powers flared. Neither crossed the invisible line that separated them.

The Princess Royal's smile vanished. "Have you forgotten where you are?"

The ladies on the other sofa gasped and whispered to each other. "How delightfully shocking."

"Behaving like spoilt children."

Nessie flinched. The purple mist intensified as the air temperature dropped.

Princess Ivandelle rose to her feet. "As a reminder of your position in our Court, I am issuing a royal decree." Her eyes encompassed the room. "Lord Karilion will escort Lady Nessandra to the ball tomorrow. Neither of them is free to dance with anyone else until she publicly apologises and seals it with a kiss."

"I'm not kissing my cousin," Nessie cried, leaping to her feet.

Karilion narrowed his eyes.

"He's only your cousin by marriage," Princess Ivandelle said. "Everyone knows that his widowed mother married your uncle. Now sit down, foolish girl."

The "foolish girl" sat, her eyes fixed on the carpet at her feet.

"Karil, go back to your seat beside the Prince." The irate royal waved her hand at him in dismissal. He obeyed. When

Karilion reached his place, Prince Braevin said something Phoena couldn't hear. Karilion shook his head, his frown deepening. He threw a troubled glance towards Phoena.

Princess Ivandelle clapped her hands. "I refuse to allow these ill-mannered children to ruin my afternoon." The maids hurried in with a refreshed tea trolley. When the servants retreated, one of the other ladies played hostess.

The Princess resumed her seat, studying Phoena over the brim of her steaming teacup. She took another sip, smiled and set down her drink. The writhing purple mist that crowned Princess Ivandelle increased Phoena's dread.

"Fee-nah," Princess Ivandelle said. "An hour ago, you promised us a story. You can't declare yourself a foundling and then disappear."

Phoena flinched. Some of her tea spilled into the saucer. Yiana gasped, and Nessie finally glanced sideways. Nessie reached for Phoena's cup, concern in her eyes. Phoena waved her away.

"I've already expl—" Nessie began.

"Miss Ashton can speak for herself," the Princess snapped. It took a few moments for that royal smile to return.

Phoena used that brief interval to pray for wisdom. She put down her cup, rose to her feet, and narrowed her focus. After bobbing politely, she found her voice. "I-I'm sorry, Your Highness, b-but the disappearance is beyond m-my comprehension."

Princess Ivandelle laughed merrily and waved her hand. An echoing ripple of laughter encircled the room. Phoena remained alert as that purple mist rushed towards her. Confident that her power was more potent, Phoena lowered her defences. Karilion had said he could still exercise self-control while bespelled...

For a few moments, the older woman's gaze enthralled Phoena – a dark intrusive presence demanding entrance to her mind. Then her defences activated themselves with a jolt. She stole a moment to remember that her guardians bestowed these protective spells. For the past fourteen years, these wards had preserved her anonymity. Now, they pushed back at the intrusion with a tenacity she had never experienced before.

A flaming barrier ignited in her mind to block the intruder. The darkness retreated, but the smile on the Princess's face didn't waver. Phoena wondered if her opponent could see the crimson flames. Before she could blink, the fire reduced to a flickering at the edge of her vision.

Princess Ivandelle tilted her head as she reached for her teacup. She added more sugar, stirring her tea with a silver spoon. Then she tapped the rim of the cup with the spoon. Once, twice, three times.

A surge of energy hit Phoena from behind.

Phoena allowed a sigh to escape. Why did everyone think an orphan girl was defenceless prey? A similar type of spell had been popular with the *Westernbrooke* students. Her confidence grew – those years of managing her reactions would prove useful. Even though these tormentors were *not* untried boys, she was confident she could outwit them without revealing her power.

A frozen numbness crept down her arm as the Princess's spell burrowed deep, yet the flickering flames in her mind didn't fade. Phoena hadn't known how to call on these defences before, yet she had always escaped. In the past, if caught by this trick, she would pretend that the spell had gone awry. Then she would hide until the effects wore off.

Another blow landed in the middle of her back. With a smile stuck on her face, Phoena kept her eyes on the Princess – she must maintain the illusion.

The icy deadening continued to spread across her body. As it crept into the muscles, she endeavoured not to shiver. When the deep chill reached Phoena's bones, fear awoke within her. In a few minutes, it would be impossible to hide the effects.

Her mind escaped in prayer.

> Aemeithriel, Creator and Sustainer, I'm afraid.
> My heart quakes within me.
> Hoyia Kaeng, You alone are King.
> You alone do I serve.
> Please draw your servant closer.
> Be my Shield and my Deliverer.
> Vathshar, Father, I call on you for help.
> I don't understand what is happening,
> and I don't know what to do.
> Teach me to be patient as I wait for you.

Phoena could feel the heat of the fire, and longed to stand closer. Was she still confident she could endure this torture without betraying her strength? As if in response to her heart's cry, a whistling noise erupted from the fireplace. Something red hot whizzed past Phoena's ear. More tiny comets quickly followed. The purple mist swatted the flaming missiles from the air. They exploded in a shower of mysterious sparks above the Princess, causing her no harm.

This pyrotechnic display was a curious distraction. Was this an answer to her prayer? Yet none of the missiles came close to hitting Princess Ivandelle. Phoena puzzled over this until she realised that her immobilised body stood between the Princess and the fireplace! The next volley hit Phoena in the back. Her defences did nothing to repel this new attack. They must be responsible but what was this supposed to achieve?

The Princess gave no visible sign that she engaged in anything other than drinking her tea. Yet the purple mist was busy. Phoena could see its energy rushing in every direction. Then as suddenly as it began, the whistling ceased. When the final sparks were extinguished, the Princess's magic surged over Phoena. The girl was careful to keep still as if incapacitated by the freezing spell.

Phoena mentally reviewed her condition. The spreading numbness had faltered. Searching for traces of the airborne embers, she found them burrowing into the frozen parts of her body. As they targeted her earlier injuries, she regained full control over the affected limbs. But she could still feel something on the surface of her back. A strange but familiar sound captured her attention. Was that the crackle of smouldering kindling just before a fire ignited?

Was she about to burst into flame?

Phoena wasn't sure if the cloud of smoke swirling around her was real. Sweat beaded on her brow as the distinctive burning smell intensified. The Princess's magic pressed closer. Phoena called moisture from the air, and then she heard a sound like water hissing on burning coals. When the mist withdrew, the attention-seeking noise had ceased, and the room was clear of smoke.

Her internal temperature continued to increase.

The wall clock chimed the quarter-hour. Princess Ivandelle sipped her tea as if there had been no great delay. The regal woman looked pensive for a few moments longer and then spoke. "Even if you can't satisfy my curiosity about today's *incidents*, you must know from where you've come? Begin with that."

Phoena opened her mouth, but not even a whisper escaped.

The Princess leaned forward. "You know there is nothing to fear from us."

Phoena breathed deeply. As she stood before the Princess, the flames within her burned brightly. Her vision blurred. Then a song flooded her mind. She recognised the voice – it belonged to the mystical healer, Ennallya. The tune had been with her all her life, but she had only learned the foreign words recently. *Shaezz vraa moem...*

Ennallya had used the song to entice Phoena from the false security of enchanted dreams. While the teenager had slumbered, her world had changed. The three young noblemen who had pledged themselves to her quest had left her, and she awoke to a new destiny.

Now, these words delivered strength and confidence. The icy bands and fiery darts lost their power to inspire fear. Phoena stood before the Princess without trembling, her uncertainty banished. The song faded to a whisper, new words forming in her mind.

"Your Highness," Phoena said, "I don't know which land I was born in, nor anything about my parents. I was orphaned as an infant. I have nothing to tell you about how or why I am under Lady Cecily's guardianship. I must have been very young when this occurred, for I have no memory of my life before I came to her."

Phoena stood taller. "Lady Cecily was charged with my upbringing. She did what was necessary to prevent me from becoming idle and ungrateful. She offers no explanation for her decisions, and I don't ask for any. I go where I'm sent, and I do as I'm told."

The words in her mind stopped abruptly, and Phoena offered no further explanation. She stood silent. There had been renewed attempts to attack her from every direction, but all had failed.

"What do we think of this foundling's tale?" the Princess asked.

"Surely there is some remembrance that might give a clue to her identity?" Duke Urdigo suggested.

"Is there?" Princess Ivandelle asked. "If there is, I command you to tell us." A surge of power accompanied those words. The Princess frowned as her directive fell short of the girl before her.

The poetic words rose to a crescendo within Phoena's mind. Her whole being urged her to sing. Obediently, she opened her mouth, and the song flowed from her:

"Shaezz vraa moem neis.

Hoovar vraa waeshaen vraagish.

Shan oshaan raeshtinn aroear, hoeiabva leststoer rayem.

Vathshar hoei ara kaeng oevar flaeth,

ae staell shaell khoei deiy.

Faenn shooth vath vrail aen thraest thraimon.

Khoe shae paell aen shoalaethnass vroet–"

"Who taught you that song?" the duke demanded, striding across the room. Phoena spun towards him. Only a cautioning word from the Princess kept him from grabbing Phoena's shoulder. Duke Urdigo towered over her, but she stood her ground. Everyone else was on their feet.

It had been fourteen years since she had last uttered a prayer in the presence of someone else. On that occasion, she had been powerless to defend herself from an angry beating. The flames behind her eyes intensified. The tingling in her fingers warned there would be a different outcome this time. "You asked if I had a remembrance."

Duke Urdigo stared at her. Time stretched as he stood frozen in place. There had been no surge of power – she could detect no other spell. Whatever had turned him into a living statue must be within him. His son, Marquis Xavier, rescued the towering man, leading him away. A blanket of silence fell as everyone waited for the elder man to regain his senses.

Five minutes later, Duke Urdigo stirred as if awakening from a deep sleep. "Impossible," he muttered.

"What's impossible?" Princess Ivandelle asked.

Phoena could see the power behind those words. Duke Urdigo shook himself. "When I'm more certain, I'll let you know."

He rose to his feet and bowed, first to the Princess and then to Phoena. "Ladies, my son and I must take our leave." Without waiting for a response, he stormed from the room. Xavier hurried to match his strides.

"I hope he doesn't expect my coachman to leave without me," Prince Braevin said. He went to the window. After a few minutes, he leaned forward and stared out. "Now, that's interesting, I've never known old Urdigo to walk anywhere.

Yet there he is marching off down the road as if an enemy pursues him."

"We've had enough excitement for one day," the Princess declared. In response, her party decamped to the coaches. Phoena stared after the vehicles until they disappeared from view. Her companions allowed her to linger for a few minutes more before the trio retreated in silence to Phoena's suite.

As soon as the door slammed behind them, Nessie asked, "What was that about?"

"Which 'that' are you asking about?" Yiana said. "The whole afternoon was impossible to—"

"Exactly," Nessie cried. "What did Lord Urdigo mean when he said Phoena was 'impossible'?"

"When we're more certain," Yiana said in a worthy imitation of Lord Urdigo, "we'll tell you."

Phoena hid her smile behind her hand, but Yiana could not hold back the laughter. Nessie frowned and then snickered.

"I thought we were really in trouble then," Yiana said when she could catch her breath.

"What makes you think we've escaped without consequences?" Phoena asked. "I don't think any of them were satisfied with the unanswered questions."

Nessie and Yiana discussed all kinds of possibilities. The clock in the reception room chimed again. "Is that the half-hour?" Yiana cried, rushing to check. "Oh, Nessie, there's no time to return to our rooms for a change of clothes before dinner!"

"Bother," said Nessie. "If Phoena's going to keep dragging us on adventures, we should keep some garments here. If only Karil hadn't marched us across the garden. These dresses are filthy."

"Have you forgotten your dip in the river?" Yiana asked.

Nessie's eyes twinkled. "Phoena, if I use my water magic to wash these dresses, could you use your fire to dry them again?"

Fifteen minutes later, all three of them were more presentable. Nessie borrowed a coloured sash and a lacy wrap from Phoena's wardrobe to imply she was wearing a new outfit. There was a spring in Nessie's step, and Yiana smiled brightly. Phoena quietly followed them down to the dining room. There was so much she needed to discuss with Cecily, and no opportunity…

CHAPTER 16:
AN ALARMING LETTER

All the students were seated, waiting for the headmistress to appear. After a longer delay than usual, one of the masters led the other teachers to the head table. "Mrs Hammersley has been unavoidably detained," he declared. When he finished his announcement, he gave the signal for service to begin.

"I bet it has something to do with what happened this afternoon," Meredith said. "Nessie, *your* cousin was wandering around the gardens with footmen in tow. They were carrying a sofa."

"*My* cousin?" Nessie said, keeping her smile pleasant. "Which one? I have so many."

"You know which one," Meredith complained. "Only Karil could get away with something like this. There's a rumour he had to leave *Westernbrooke* in disgrace for taking liberties with the servants."

"Don't believe everything you hear," Nessie said. "The truth about Karil is never as interesting as the gossip."

"There's something to this story," Meredith insisted. "None of the *Westernbrooke* servants will talk about it. I'm going to ask him at your mother's ball."

"If he's there," Nessie said, playing with her spoon. "I hear he has annoyed the Princess Royal. If he's sensible, he'll stay away until she's forgiven him."

Yiana choked on her soup. Phoena thumped Yiana on the back before passing her the water glass. At that moment, there was a movement at the main entrance. The footman opened the door. Everyone craned to see who the latecomer was. Mrs Hammersley entered, accompanied by Phoena's godmother Cecily. The two women walked towards Nessie's table. A hush swept across the dining room.

Dragging herself to her feet, Phoena forgot to breathe. Nessie and Yiana leapt up, wrapping their arms around her.

"It wasn't Phoena's fault," Nessie began.

"Be quiet," snapped Mrs Hammersley. "Miss Ashton, your guardian requires you to leave with her immediately."

"Will she be back?" Yiana asked.

"Of course she'll be back," the headmistress said, but she didn't sound convinced.

"Phoena's education remains a priority," Cecily said. "Come along, young lady." Without waiting for a reply, Cecily retraced her path. Phoena and her two friends hurried after her guardian. The footman opened the door to let them pass. When they were in the hallway, Cecily frowned at Nessie and Yiana. "Go back to your dinner."

"Not until you explain why you're taking Phoena," Nessie said.

Cecily sighed. "Come as far as the coach."

When they were outside, Cecily stopped. "Lady Cascade, you should have asked my permission before parading Phoena before royalty."

"I didn't think—" Nessie protested.

"Of course you didn't," Cecily agreed. "That's one of your character flaws. Apply yourself to remedy that. The Princess Royal is most displeased."

"Who told you that?"

"Lord Karilion reported to Lord Westernbrooke as soon as he returned."

"Is that why you're here?" Yiana asked. "Is Phoena in danger?"

Cecily considered her reply. "Phoena needs time to prepare."

"Prepare for what?" Nessie asked.

A wry smile appeared on Cecily's face. "Lord Karilion was not the only bearer of news." She withdrew a white envelope from her pocket.

"What?" Nessie cried.

"Who?" Yiana said at the same time.

Cecily handed the letter to Phoena. "Read it aloud."

"Dear Lady de Montnoir, I request your permission to call on your protégé—"

"Let me see!" Nessie screeched, wrestling the paper from Phoena's hand. "Oh, no. It's signed: Xavier, Marquis of Umbryden. He wants to marry Phoena!"

The pavement beneath Phoena's feet shifted as darkness called to her.

"It says nothing of marriage," Cecily said sternly, grasping Phoena's arm.

"That's the only reason he'd visit," Nessie replied. "Lady Cecily, you can't let her marry him. He has a cruel reputation."

"Who are you to tell me what I should or shouldn't do?" Cecily said. "I can only imagine what was said and done to bring Phoena to his attention."

"It wasn't Phoena's fault," Yiana said.

"No," cried Nessie. "It wasn't. She portrayed herself as dull and uninteresting. It was Karil and I who made a scene. Oh, Phoena, I'm so sorry."

"It's too late to be sorry," Cecily said. "There is much to be done if we are to manage the consequences."

"What are your plans?" Yiana asked.

"Wait and see." Cecily frowned at Yiana. "You are attending Nessandra's ball tomorrow?"

Yiana blushed. "I-I wasn't–"

"Nonsense," Cecily snapped. "Phoena needs you. My driver will collect you tomorrow afternoon." She pushed Phoena towards the open door of the coach. "Come along, troublesome child. There's no need for us to loiter here."

"I still have questions," Yiana said as the coachman closed the door.

Cecily leaned out the window. "Look to the mirror."

"But we can't go to Phoena's room without her," Yiana protested.

Cecily dismissed her concerns with a wave. "When the pair of you retire from dinner, you will find your possessions are now in Phoena's suite. I suggested to Mrs Hammersley that Phoena might elope– The headmistress was quick to agree that she must have someone with her at all times."

"Elope!" Nessie cried. "Not with Xavier – she's not!"

"Of course not," Cecily frowned. "But that impossibility was more believable than the real reason."

"Which is?" Nessie asked.

Cecily gave the signal, and the coachman cracked his whip. As the wheels began to roll along the driveway, Cecily shook her head. "Go back to your dinner. Consider the change to your situation. I will talk with you later."

CHAPTER 17:
LIGHTING THE FIRE

The following evening, Phoena sat with her godparents in Lord Westernbrooke's enclosed coach. She leaned out the open window, eager for a glimpse of Nessie's family home. The curved driveway shielded the house from the road.

It was past sunset. They must be late, but there were other vehicles ahead of them. When their coach rolled forward again, her vigilance brought results. Nessie's home was a grander stone building than Cecily's Sumnarscote mansion. This evening, lights burned in every window. Uniformed footmen opened coach doors, escorting guests up the broad stairs.

"Lean back into the coach," Cecily growled, "and stop pulling at your dress."

Phoena flopped onto her seat, but her restless hands refused to behave.

"If you don't desist, I'll put a command spell on you."

The nervous teenager bit back a retort. They both knew that Cecily's spell wouldn't work. Her godmother had already experienced that kind of failure during her attempt to style Phoena's long hair. The hairbrush had flown from Cecily's hand, shattering a window on its way out of the house. Her godmother narrowly avoided the metal hairpins which shot past in pursuit.

Phoena gave the dress one last tug before folding her hands in her lap. "I feel naked. This dress doesn't have enough fabric in the bodice."

"Foolish child, do you think this is your dressmaker's first ball gown?" Cecily complained. "If you're so worried, use your defences to adhere the dress to your skin. But be quick. There's only one coach ahead of us."

Phoena closed her eyes and pressed her hands to the front neckline. Sparks fired from her fingertips without direction. "Oh, it stings!" What was happening? The pain suggested sharp needles were at work.

Opening her eyes brought a revelation. "Cecily," she cried, throwing her hands over her face. "I can't see anything but flames."

What terrible timing! After her encounter with the Princess Royal, Phoena had not been able to coax this new kind of fire to reappear. She had wanted to show her guardians so they could teach her how to control it. After listening to her account, Cecily had described the phenomenon as "second flame" – another mystery on a growing list of unanswered questions. Hopefully, Yiana would know something...

But first, Phoena had to get out of the coach – the "second flame" had blinded her.

"Keep still," Cecily said. Instead of leaning closer, her godmother sounded further away. "Take your hands away from your face. Westy, have you seen anything like this before? Her skin has turned red like a cooked lobster. And she's hot! The metal brace on the window has started to glow. I'm surprised she hasn't already ignited."

Phoena spluttered. *Ignited!*

"Cecily, you know that without smoke, there's no danger," Lord Westernbrooke said. "You're panicking the child. I'll get out and distract the footman while you deal with this. Perhaps you can throw a cloak over her?"

Phoena called moisture from the air to cool her face, and the effort constrained her tears. Locking her fingers together, she portrayed an outward serenity as she waited for her heart rate to slow. "I'm sorry for overreacting."

"Don't apologise," Cecily said, passing Phoena a heavy cloak. "It was my suggestion that triggered this reaction. I should have known better..."

"I can see again," Phoena said, pulling the hood over her head. "I think it's safe." She cautiously reached for the door, watching the timber for any sign of smoke. With a sigh, she pushed the door open.

She hesitated for a moment before she accepted Lord Westernbrooke's hand. The footman sniffed – helping her from the coach was *his* job. After Phoena stumbled from the coach, the footman pushed forward to assist Cecily. Phoena was thankful for the brief reprieve. The ground rocked beneath her feet, and she caught her godfather's arm.

"Let's get her inside so I can be certain," Cecily said when she joined them. "There are too many shadows here."

"Certain of what?" Westy asked.

The footman hovered. Cecily waved him onward before she responded. "Shhh."

Lord Westernbrooke stiffened but asked nothing more. Phoena smiled beneath her hood. For all his bluster, Westy was Cecily's obedient lamb. Under her godmother's direction, he shepherded the teenager inside.

"A private room," Cecily demanded as soon as they passed through the main door. The footman led the way. "You wait here," she told Westy. The two women entered a small chamber.

With the door closed, Phoena lowered the hood. "Won't the footman wonder what we're doing?"

"Haven't you learned anything from your time at the College?" Cecily asked, discarding the cloak. "An inter-generational confrontation upon arrival is not uncommon. But usually it's the parent who complains about a too-revealing costume."

Phoena blushed as Cecily thrust her towards the wall mirror. They studied her reflection. The intense redness to her face and neck was fading. Phoena stepped closer to the silvered surface. A lacy red extension had appeared around her gown's neckline.

Removing one of her long gloves, Phoena rubbed at the lace on her chest. Her fingers detected nothing but bare flesh. The dark red lines penetrated her skin, like exquisite crimson ink on parchment. Cecily spun her around while Phoena studied the reflection. The design was a uniform width around the top of her gown. The filigreed pattern was intricate, the breadth of her palm. She pushed aside one narrow sleeve and stared at the concealed markings on her skin.

Without a word, Cecily unfastened the gown at the back. Phoena clutched the fabric to her chest as the liberated dress slipped towards the floor. On her back, the skin markings continued as low as she could see – at least to her waist. Only the skin above her shoulders was untainted.

"I don't think you need to worry about protecting your modesty," Cecily said. "This gives the illusion that you are wearing an undergarment of the finest lace. As long as no-one touches the lace, you will be safe." Cecily refastened the dress and adjusted the fit.

"How long will it last?" Phoena asked, tracing a flame-shaped design with her fingertip.

"It looks permanent," Cecily told her. "I've seen this kind of skin decoration before, in a distant land. It's called a tattoo. Ink is delivered into the lower layers of the skin using fine needles." She shook her head. "Stop rubbing at your shoulder, and put your glove back on."

Phoena unfastened Yiana's bracelet to replace the glove. With the gemstones again on her wrist, she admired the fire-altered stones. Together with her other trinkets, they were a comforting reminder – she was not alone on this undefined quest. Karilion's bangle adorned her other wrist. In the dressing room's candlelight, it was unremarkable. Yet in the darkened coach, this dull metal band had glowed with a mysterious luminescence.

She leaned closer to the mirror. Baraapa's medallion no longer seemed out of place. It bore a similar design to the skin markings. An avalanche of questions flooded her mind.

Phoena glanced at Cecily. Expecting no satisfaction from her godmother, the girl chewed her lip. If Baraapa were here, he wouldn't hesitate to give his opinion about recent events. Tears sprang to her eyes as a peculiar pain pierced her heart. She turned her head away from Cecily.

A surge of energy from within the mirror took her by surprise. Instead of her reflection, she saw a group of men seated around a fire. One by one, they stopped talking and stared at her.

"What foolishness is this?" Cecily asked. "How did you make this ordinary mirror behave like that?"

"I-I d-didn't—"

Cecily raised her hand to erase the scene, but as the vision wavered, one of the men strode directly towards them. He was wearing only a waistcoat and loose-fitting pants. The warrior's bulging chest muscles glowed like copper in the firelight, and his hair was a vibrant orange.

Phoena gasped. "Baraapa!"

"My Lady," the massive warrior replied with a generous bow. "You seem as surprised by this visitation as I." He nodded towards her godmother. "Lady Cecily, I presume her magic is as unpredictable as ever."

"More problematic than I expected," Cecily said. "If only you were here... I could use both your cleverness and your supernatural strength to keep her out of trouble."

Baraapa frowned. His mouth opened as if to ask a question.

"No time," her godmother said.

Suddenly his image was gone. The abrupt disappearance wounded Phoena. She pretended to adjust her layered petticoats. The skirt of the forest-green gown billowed from the tight waist. Satisfied, she rechecked the bodice. The red decoration at the neckline did nothing to hide her feminine curves. Her face flushed, and she glanced towards the brown cloak.

Cecily shook her head and hung the cloak on one of the wall hooks. "Leave this here. The time for pretending there is anything plain or unattractive about you has passed." Her godmother opened the small purse that hung at her wrist. "I brought a length of ribbon, and more pins, in case your hair decided to behave when we got here. I will leave you to fix it yourself."

Accepting the ribbon from her godmother's hand, Phoena drew her hair up. Cecily helped her tie the dark locks in place. Phoena adjusted the position of the wave-shaped pin and then added the extra hairpins. With her hair piled high, she arranged a few trailing curls around her neck. She clasped both hands to her chest, wondering if her hair might rebel. Her fingers wrapped around the dragon brooch her champion Oramis had gifted her.

When nothing went awry, she smiled and spun towards Cecily. "How do I look?"

"You look lovely, dear Lady," a voice said from behind her. "Command me, and I will fly across the world to be with you."

Phoena froze. Cecily pushed the girl aside and glared at the mirror.

"Oramis," her godmother said. "I've warned you not to make idle promises."

The grinning foreigner bowed graciously. "Lady Cecily," blond Oramis said. "You look charming this evening. Are we attending a ball?"

"Your name wasn't on the invitation," Cecily replied, "but you do have a reputation as a party-crasher." She gestured at the mirror, and his image shimmered. "Phoena is making her debut this evening."

The vision faded as his final words hung in the air. "Save a dance for me."

"He won't really come, will he?" Phoena asked.

"Don't concern yourself with Oramis."

CHAPTER 18:
A GRAND ENTRANCE

Cecily ushered Phoena into the hallway. Lord Westernbrooke was deep in conversation with another older gentleman. He only paused when Cecily stood directly in front of him. "Is she—" Westy asked.

"See for yourself," Cecily replied, ushering Phoena forward.

"*This* is your goddaughter?" the other man asked. His smile brightened, and he reached for Phoena's hand. "You never mentioned her beauty." He planted a kiss on her glove. "No wonder you've been hiding her." Cecily removed Phoena's fingers from his firm grip. He grinned. "Before the night is out, I'm sure she'll have many suitors. Play your cards well, Westernbrooke. I predict your investment in raising this young woman will be repaid a hundredfold."

"Indeed?" Lord Westernbrooke grumbled. "I hadn't considered that possibility."

"If only I were a few years younger—"

Westy marched her away without waiting for the man to finish his remark. "I'm not convinced she is old enough for this," he muttered. Neither of his companions gave a reply.

Too soon, the trio stood in the antechamber before the ballroom. The manservant stationed there wore a more elaborate uniform. They waited while the preceding group descended the short staircase.

Down below, Nessie's parents welcomed their guests. When the nobles ahead of them were halfway down, the herald signalled Phoena's group forward. Phoena was thankful for the etiquette rehearsed before each dance lesson, or she wouldn't have known what to do. It was easy to pretend she was ready. Lord Westernbrooke offered Cecily his bent right arm and she rested her gloved hand near his elbow.

"Lord Westernbrooke and Lady de Montnoir."

Without checking to see that she was following, the pair began to descend. Phoena took a step forward, but the herald held up his hand. She frowned as he barred her way, leaving her stranded and alone.

Phoena's eyes drifted over the ballroom. From her vantage point, she caught a glimpse of a magnificent fireplace positioned on a side wall. The bright fire called to her. She dragged her eyes back to the scene at the foot of the stairs where her godparents were being welcomed by Nessie and her parents. Yiana waved in the background. Phoena drew comfort from that sensible friend's presence. If only she were up here.

The original plan had been for Yiana to escort Phoena down the stairs. That arrangement had gone out the window with the errant hairbrush. Each invitation prescribed the time for arrival, so Yiana had travelled alone in Cecily's coach. Lord Westernbrooke's coach was the logical option once they were delayed. As a member of the King's Council, he was much later in the schedule.

A crowd gathered around the base of the stairs, guests waiting to welcome the royal party. Phoena took a half-step sideways. Perhaps the herald could be convinced to forget she was here? She peered at him through her lashes. The herald shuffled, looking over her shoulder to the next person in the line.

The floorboards creaked, and a figure loomed over her. She held her breath. A man wearing robes appeared beside her. She knew only two people who wore these unfashionable robes, and the safe one was down below.

"You've become separated from your guardians," Duke Urdigo said. His voice was too close. She blinked in his direction as the Duke brought her arm into the crook of his own. His fingers closed over her gloved hand, trapping her beside him. "Allow me to escort you, Miss Ashton." His smile didn't waver, but his eyes watched for her response. "You can save me having to face our hostess alone."

Was there a way to extricate herself from Duke Urdigo's company without a public scandal? Cecily was speaking with Nessie's mother, seemingly oblivious to Phoena's dilemma.

"Duke Urdigo and Miss Ashton," the herald declared. Phoena's feet propelled her forward. Unlike her dance partners at College, Duke Urdigo was in no hurry for the procession to end.

"You are ill at ease with me," he said. "Perfectly understandable after the way I behaved yesterday." She remained quiet. He patted her hand. "You're a pretty little thing. I don't think I noticed that before. If I were forty years younger, you might have something to worry about. But I'm sure there'll be no lack of eligible men lining up to fill your dance card."

They were halfway down the stairs, and she was still flustered.

"Hmmm – are you shy, or simply awaiting instructions? I can see old Westernbrooke glaring up at me. I'm not on his list of potential suitors. Evidently, he wasn't expecting anyone to separate you from his guardianship so easily. I'm tempted to pretend there's more to this conversation, if only to watch his reaction."

Phoena's heart quaked. "Please don't."

"The maiden has found her voice," he chuckled. "What did Westernbrooke say when you told him about your afternoon's adventures? I'm more than a little weary of the Princess Royal's tricks. One day, someone is going to be *seriously* hurt. I wish I could tell her to act her age – she's only a year younger than her brother, the King. At forty-four, she should know better."

"We've arrived," Phoena said as her feet touched the marble floor. He stopped moving forward, even though they were still a few paces from their hosts. The teenager took this as a signal to make her escape. Yet he pulled her closer until their faces were almost touching.

"You need to exercise care," Duke Urdigo said in a low voice. "I can feel the magic sizzling through your arm."

Phoena's tension escalated. She glanced around. Cecily was fast approaching. Others at the edge of the crowd were whispering.

The Duke took a step back, bowed over her hand and kissed it. "I wish you luck, Miss Ashton. You're going to need it. Your power reminds me of someone I once knew. Things didn't end well for them. Be careful with your alliances."

A question escaped her. "Did you ask your son to send that message?"

"Xavier?" He frowned. "I know nothing of a message." He scanned the crowd. "He's not here to meet me. The King must have summoned him." He stared into her eyes. "My son makes his own decisions – except when he's under orders from the Princess. Make sure you mention that to your guardians. Whatever scheme is in operation, I'm not involved."

Cecily guided Phoena and Yiana to a row of chairs in an isolated corner. She ordered them to stay there.

The longed-for fireplace was across the room. Phoena could not hear what her godparents discussed, even though they were only a few steps away. A flickering secrecy spell hovered over them. A glance around the ballroom revealed more than one kind of enchantment at work among the guests. She looked back to her godparents. Lord Westernbrooke was becoming increasingly stern.

"Are you sure Duke Urdigo said his son was under orders from the Princess?" Yiana asked. "I can't imagine what Her Highness expects to gain. Wasn't it sufficient that Karil behaved like an absolute idiot towards you?"

"I was hoping you might know the answer."

"Look out, here comes another hopeful suitor."

It took a few minutes to explain to the eager young man that Cecily had custody of Phoena's dance card. Yiana fanned herself with the one she held. Phoena nodded towards her friend. The youth politely asked Yiana to add his name.

"At least one of us is doing well out of this," Yiana chortled. "I've never had so many offers. I'll have to make sure I always bring you with me."

"Why hasn't the dancing started?"

"We have to wait for the royal party to arrive. They're always last. Anyone not here by then will be refused entry."

"Karilion isn't here. Nessie must be pleased that she's ruined his social life. It looks as if all the local nobility have crammed into this ballroom."

"He will probably arrive with the royals," Yiana said. "Nessie's going to have a miserable time if he doesn't show. Her mother was furious with Nessie when she heard of the Princess's decree. There's no dancing for our friend without him. She's under strict instructions to apologise to her cousin at the first opportunity."

"Do you think she will?"

"I'm not sure. Her mother's matchmaking efforts are futile if Nessie can only dance with Karil. I've already pointed out two likely prospects. But Nessie needs to stay on the right side of Princess Ivandelle. There's her future at Court to consider."

Trumpets sounded, and every conversation ended. The herald began the introductions as the royal party emerged on the landing. The girls were far enough away that Yiana could add pertinent information. Phoena thought it took less time for the whole party to descend than for her torturous promenade.

As Yiana predicted, Karilion was with them. He had the honour of escorting Princess Ivandelle on the stairs. Among the twenty in the Princess Royal's entourage, Phoena recognised the three ladies who attended afternoon tea. The group flowed down the stairs so closely behind the Princess they could have been a rainbow-hued train for her yellow dress. When everyone had passed by Nessie's family, the royal party did not spread out across the room. Instead, they turned to face the stairs.

A spontaneous gasp echoed through the room. Before it faded, the trumpets sounded a longer fanfare. "Oh! I didn't know *he* was coming." Yiana dragged Phoena to her feet and dove into the crowd. Phoena's godparents appeared beside them. The people around them grumbled as they moved through until they recognised Lord Westernbrooke. Then everyone hastened to let the massive dignitary and his companions move into the front row. By the time the trumpet chorus ended, the two girls had a prime position.

A short man in ornate robes appeared at the top of the stairs. An oppressive magical cloud came into the room with him. He wore a crown on his grey head – he looked ancient, many years older than forty-five. The chains of office around his neck seemed an impossible weight for such a frail man to bear.

"His Majesty, King Andressan, Lord of the Western Empire, Commander of the Five Seas."

A shout erupted from the crowd. "Hail to the King! Long live the King! Hail to the King!"

Phoena caught her breath. Plumes of coloured magic whizzed here and there. Exploding sparks and bolts of lightning enlivened the room. A web of protection wove itself between Westy and Cecily, forming a barrier around the four of them. Phoena looked longingly towards the fireplace.

The burdened King raised his arm in acknowledgement. Two richly dressed noblemen stepped forward from the shadows behind him.

The herald spoke again. "This evening, His Majesty is attended by Xavier, Marquis of Umbryden – and His Royal Highness, Prince Braevin."

The two "attendants" did not greet the assembly. Instead, they stood on either side of the King. He wrapped an arm around each of them, and then his whole body sagged. The two strong men bore his weight, raising him to his full height.

In horrified fascination, Phoena watched the monarch take a faltering step. His legs bent unnaturally, and his upper body lurched sideways. Phoena gasped. Her reaction drew attention from the nearby spectators.

She shut out their presence, focusing on the three men descending the stairs. The lines on the King's face expressed his pain. His progress was distressing to watch. Phoena edged forward, but Cecily pulled her back.

Phoena pushed against the constraint. Her power increased, and she started to float. Yiana wrapped her arms around Phoena and pulled her back to the marble floor.

"Not now," Westy growled. "There are too many people here."

CHAPTER 19:
A BROKEN KING

"What happened to the King?" Phoena asked.

"A hunting accident shattered his legs when he was young. Nobody expected him to live long enough to claim the crown."

Phoena blinked away tears. "Isn't there anything that can ease his pain?"

"What can you see?" Cecily asked. "All I detect are the usual defensive spells that the royals employ."

"There's a black cloud pressing down over him. I can't tell if it's supposed to be protecting him or if it's attacking him. The lightning bolts are draining the energy away from him. If it doesn't stop, he's going to die."

Yiana and Cecily jumped, and their eyes locked.

Lord Westernbrooke scanned the room.

"Be careful not to mention that again," her godfather advised her.

"Wait for me here," he said to Cecily. "I will take my position in the receiving line and see what I can discover."

He shouldered his way towards the Princess Royal's party. There was movement at the foot of the stairs, and four servants entered carrying an elaborate throne. Xavier and Prince Braevin lowered the weary King onto the throne. He slumped in silence, his head bowed.

The crowd waited.

Nessie's parents approached the throne. Xavier spoke to the King, and he raised his head. The host and hostess bowed, then Nessie stepped forward to join them.

For a moment, the King pulled himself upright. The atmosphere around him lightened. Nessie's laughter rang out as she lifted her blue locks for his inspection. Phoena wished she could hear the fanciful explanation.

The King listened for a few minutes, but then his eyes closed. Xavier waved Nessie and her parents away. They walked backwards, even though he no longer acknowledged their presence.

The servants carried the enthroned sovereign towards the fireplace. From this position, King Andressan seemed to have a good view of the ballroom. Yet his throne was sufficiently out of the way that it did not intrude upon the dance floor.

The crowd shuffled to accommodate his new position. The orchestra tuned their instruments, and music filled the air. Couples greeted each other throughout the room, but the dancing did not begin. Princess Ivandelle ushered one of her ladies into the King's presence. Phoena watched the magical energy ebb and flow. She longed to be closer. Instead, Cecily pulled her away to a secluded corner.

With a sigh, Phoena settled for an occasional glimpse of the King. Guests jostled for position, but Lord Westernbrooke remained in prominence among the members of the royal Court. Nessie stood arguing with her parents at the foot of the stairs. Karilion had joined them. He said something, and his blue-haired cousin turned away. He followed her as she pushed through the crowd.

Phoena felt torn. Which was more important? Addressing her growing concern about Nessie's volatility? Or satisfying her curiosity over King Andressan? "Why is everyone hovering around the throne?"

"The King is supposed to choose a partner and lead the first dance," Yiana told her. "He doesn't like any of his sister's recommendations."

"How can he dance when he's so broken?"

"See that gentleman waiting on the other side of the fireplace. He's the royal apothecary. He's prepared a potion for the King to drink. This makes his legs strong."

"If there's a potion, why isn't he well?" Phoena asked.

"Each time he uses it, he requires a more potent dose. And the effect is weaker. It's been six months since he last attended a ball. That night, he barely lasted to the final stanza of the opening tune."

"Then why doesn't he let someone stand-in for him?"

"When he isn't here," Yiana said, "the Princess Royal takes his place. But there have been rumours that he's too ill to reign. The King's Council asked him to attend this ball and prove the naysayers wrong."

"He's here. Why does he have to dance?"

"The King is the centre of Court life. If he can't dance, that introduces other doubts. What else is he unable to do?"

CHAPTER 20:
A FAILED ENCHANTMENT

Angry voices carried across the crowded room. Phoena craned her neck to see. "That's the Princess Royal. Why is Xavier arguing with her?"

The raised voices suddenly fell silent. A murmur swept through the crowd. The people standing on either side of Lord Westernbrooke cleared a space around him. Xavier spoke to him for a moment before her godfather waved in Cecily's direction.

"Westy is signalling for us," Cecily said to Phoena. "Keep quiet unless you're addressed." She took Phoena by the arm and propelled her forward. The other guests stepped out of their way.

"Phoena is to be introduced to the King," Westy said when they reached him.

Phoena glanced at Xavier and was unable to look away. He smiled as a web of darkness reached for her, and she fought the impulse to walk towards him. His hungry expression declared he already saw her as his possession. Phoena's heart pounded and the flames behind her eyes flared to break his spell. She waved her hand to fan her red face while taking a step away. She was careful not to make eye contact again.

The sparks at Phoena's fingertips flashed a warning. Across the room, the fire popped and crackled. Cecily leaned closer. Phoena almost missed the whispered warning. "Control your power."

Phoena bowed her head before the Marquis. "I'm not worthy of an introduction to the King. I'm only a foolish schoolgirl."

"What you are is a mystery," Xavier said, raising her chin. She blinked rapidly. He smiled. "The Princess Royal thinks you may be a useful distraction."

She froze. Xavier whispered in her ear. "Don't worry about Ivandelle. I can protect you from her. When we are alone, I look forward to uncovering *all* your secrets."

"The King grows impatient," Lord Westernbrooke said. He nodded to Cecily, who propelled Phoena across the open space. Phoena glanced over her shoulder. Her godfather was glaring at Xavier. "If you don't hurry, I will introduce her myself."

Xavier strode past Phoena towards the King with Lord Westernbrooke matching each step.

The broken sovereign shifted on his throne, shuffling for a more comfortable position. His pain must be intense because his breathing ceased for a few moments. The Marquis watched for a signal.

King Andressan's grey eyes locked on Phoena. A glance was enough for her to read mistrust and uncertainty on his pain-weary face. His thin beard was scraggly; there was nothing to suggest the handsome youth whose portrait hung at the *Westernbrooke Academy*.

Up close, the dark magical storm that hung over him was mesmerising.

Xavier called her godfather forward. "Your Majesty, Lord Westernbrooke, a longstanding member of your Council. He served both your father and your grandfather before him." The elder statesman bowed stiffly. "There has never been any question of *his* loyalty."

A murmur of discontent came from the Princess's direction. The King shifted in his seat.

The introductions continued. "May I present Lady de Montnoir. She has recently returned to your domain from places afar. I believe she has taken up residence at Sumnarscote." Cecily dropped into a deep curtsey. The King barely glanced in her direction.

Cecily gently nudged her goddaughter forward, smiling as if this was a great honour. Phoena studied that ominous storm cloud and her feet refused to move. Xavier huffed his displeasure and stood behind her. With a hand on each of her shoulders, the Marquis shoved her forward. She almost stumbled, and his fingers tightened their grip.

Xavier pressed his body against her. A jolt of energy leapt between them, awakening her fear. His cruel fingers stroked her bare skin, trailing magic as they went. "And this young woman," Xavier said, "is their goddaughter, Miss Ashton." As he spoke, a spiral of dark magic wrapped itself like a collar around her neck. "An orphan, she is under their shared guardianship."

Phoena ground her heel into the floor while her eyes searched for an escape route. Did Xavier think she would do nothing while he attempted to enslave her? She prepared to strike him, intending to flee before her defences activated themselves.

King Andressan straightened in his seat and leaned forward. The dark cloud over him intensified. She was almost sure he could see Xavier's spell. He raised his hand. Hope blossomed that he would come to her aid. But his words were not what she expected. "The guardians can go."

Her disappointment was quickly followed by indignation and dismay. Cecily and Lord Westernbrooke withdrew without hesitation. They gave her no signal to direct her actions as they retreated towards Yiana. Nessie and Karilion pushed separately through the crowd to intercept them. Cecily shushed their protests, guiding everyone out of view towards their secluded corner.

Phoena faced the sovereign again. She waited as if she was helpless against Xavier's spell. King Andressan frowned. "Come closer," he commanded. Phoena raised her foot. The invisible band constricted around her throat. She lifted her hand, but before she could grip the spell, the King flicked his wrist. A bolt of energy zapped the band, and it snapped into non-existence. "Xavier, I release you from your obligations."

"But Your Majesty—"

"I grow weary of your presence. Tell my sister that I am not so close to death that I don't recognise her meddling."

"I can assure you—"

"Enough! Your petty jealousy demeans you. Why do you envy a dying man the company of a beautiful woman? When I am gone, you can play your childish games, but not while I am here. Leave me."

Xavier did not rejoin Princess Ivandelle and her courtiers. Instead, he strode towards the refreshment tables at the opposite end of the room.

Phoena watched until he passed the fireplace. The flames called to her, chasing away the chill from her heart. Her breathing slowed.

"Come closer," King Andressan said.

She obeyed. Inexplicably, the flames from her inner fire faded to nothing in the King's presence. Did this mean that he wasn't a threat?

"How old are you?"

"Seventeen, Your Majesty."

"You look much older. It is a shame that Xavier has claimed you."

"I am not an object for him to claim."

"You think you can withstand his magic? You were powerless against the spell that was binding you to him. A few minutes longer, and you would have been under his command."

"Nobody commands me, Your Majesty."

A loud buzz swept the crowd. Everyone had an opinion about the way she addressed the King.

"Insolent girl!"

"Outrageous!"

"Silence!" the King shouted. "If you distract me again, I will banish everyone from the room." He glared at Phoena. "I am your King. It is my right to command you."

"I would willingly serve you."

"I have enough servants. Why do I need a foolish child like you?"

"You're the one who summoned me."

CHAPTER 21:
AN EVIL POTION

Phoena waited for the King to respond to her statement. Suddenly, he groaned, and his fingers clawed the arms of the throne. His face crumpled with pain and his lower body writhed as a spasm seized him.

"What kind of sorcery is this?" someone shouted.

A courtier drew his sword. "That girl has bewitched the King!"

Someone screamed while others fled from the approaching swordsman. A few spectators crept closer.

"Hold your sword," Prince Braevin shouted. He stood guard over Phoena, daring anyone to touch her. Marquis Xavier moved in her direction and the prince waved him back.

A weasel-faced man approached the throne and peered into King Andressan's eyes. Yiana had earlier identified him as the king's apothecary. He scanned the air around the agonised man. Finally, he circled Phoena several times. He poked her with a polished wooden stick. The apothecary frowned at the implement. He shook it several times and repeated the process. "I can detect no sorcery, Prince Braevin. This girl presents no threat to His Majesty."

King Andressan sat rigid until the spasms eased, squinting at Phoena. The cloud around him stretched towards her. Phoena remained vigilant. Blue sparks neutralised any dark lightning that came too near.

"Then what's wrong with the King?" Prince Braevin asked.

The apothecary shrugged. "Nothing more than the usual

complaint. His Majesty need only consume the potion I have prepared, and he will have relief."

"Give it to him, then."

Someone handed the apothecary a jewel-encrusted goblet. As he carried the golden cup with reverence, a foul miasma rose from the potion. Phoena wrinkled her nose at the stench. Part of her Fellowship training required her to study from the apothecary pharmacopoeia. She could accurately detect at least a dozen deadly toxins by scent alone. She frowned, bunching the fabric of her dress between her fingers. Did she know enough to trust her judgement?

When the apothecary was beside Phoena, the King stopped his progress. "I will receive the potion from her hand."

The apothecary hesitated. "Pardon, Your Majesty?"

"Give the cup to the girl."

Prince Braevin took the potion from the apothecary's hand. He passed it to Phoena with a warning: "Make sure you don't spill a drop."

To emphasise his threat, he withdrew a short dagger from his belt.

Her trembling hands accepted the goblet as her heart raced. With great effort, she erased all emotion from her face. After she wrapped her fingers around the bowl, she closed her eyes. Her mind, enhanced by her defences, worked feverishly. This potion was a tricky balance of science and magic. Before she could do anything else, she must identify the different components.

Phoena breathed in – the pungent fumes made her eyes water. This was not the first time she had been set an impossible challenge. The Fellowship favoured practical experiments to test her skills. But in those cases, an expert would intervene if she made a mistake. Nobody was ever in danger.

Now she understood why her trainers had spurned traditional methods. When she had mastered the basic apothecary skills, they challenged her with more complex potions. There had been an urgency to these lessons. The Fellowship had not explained their expectations. They only demanded that she manipulate increasingly complex chemical compounds without hesitation.

At first, she had been slow, but they had dealt with that too. One day, Cecily had grabbed the incomplete solution from Phoena's hand and swallowed it whole. Her godmother had almost perished. The horror of that memory fuelled the urgency of today's task. The flashing blue sparks at her fingertips moved at unprecedented speed. Compounds divided, elements separated and then recombined to become something new.

If only she had more time. She focused on the layers of spells: one for blocking pain, another for strength to endure torment. Here was a strange one – the ability to fly twisted into something that lightened physical burdens. It was bound to an enchantment for dulling of the senses. But what was this – hidden deep beneath the others? A powerful curse that promised a slow and painful death – overlaid with discouragement and despair.

At the edge of her mind, she sensed the King's dark energy wrap itself around her like a heavy cloak. She almost dropped the cup, but he did not attempt to impede her progress. After tightening her grip, she urged herself to work faster. She had only a few moments if she was to save the King. When she opened her eyes, the surface of the potion bubbled and hissed. She could barely see King Andressan through the steam rising from the concoction.

The onlookers pulled back to avoid the stench.

The Prince coughed and rubbed his face. "You said she had no sorcery. This potion has never done this before."

The apothecary attempted to remove the cup from her hands.

"Bring it here, girl!" King Andressan roared, almost toppling forward from his throne. She took a long stride, catching his weight with her shoulder. He fell heavily against her. His heartbeat was erratic as she eased him back into his seat. "You're stronger than you look," he said, fear and wonder in his eyes.

She made no reply. His arm wrapped around her waist while the other hand grasped the stem of the goblet. He stared into her eyes as he pushed the cup to her lips. "Drink."

Cries of protest erupted behind her, but she was beyond their help. Phoena opened her mouth and took a large sip. She swallowed and gagged. The bitter concoction burnt her tongue, and a small amount dribbled down her chin. While her body reacted spontaneously to the liquid, her educated tastebuds worked hard. She groaned – the remedy was only half-done. Should she divert her energy away from the potion towards saving herself?

She wrestled with the temptation to pitch the potion to the floor. Perhaps King Andressan could read her mind? He snatched away the cup and held it close to his chest. "Get her some water."

Phoena lifted her head, grateful for the diversion. "Wait – I only need a minute – to catch my breath." She grimaced and wiped her chin with her glove. "That potion's disgusting."

"She's done something to my potion!" the apothecary cried. He tried to retrieve the goblet from the King's hand. Prince Braevin and Xavier wrestled him away.

"What makes you think she's changed your potion?" King Andressan asked.

"Look at her. Unharmed, unchanged, unaffected! Even that small mouthful should have contained enough..." He stopped suddenly, turning pale.

"Enough what?" the King asked, peering into the goblet. He sniffed at the contents.

"You spoke too soon," Princess Ivandelle said, appearing beside the apothecary. The two noblemen released him. "I can sense a change in the girl. Stand back and give the spell room to work."

As the crowd shuffled to get a better view, a solution to Phoena's situation flared into existence. The idea sprang from her "easy victim" days at the *Academy*. She was confident in her ability to conceal the effects of a spell. Now she must convince this crowd of the exact opposite. These people would believe the impossible when magic was involved. Their response to Nessie's blue hair was evidence of that. Phoena reflected on the active enchantments in the potion. The twisted flying spell gave her inspiration.

Phoena's body became the epicentre for a hot wind. The breeze buffeted those closest to her. A collective shout arose from the spectators as they shuffled backwards. She moderated the intensity, restricting the gusts to the magically sensitive royals nearby.

The Princess held her ground, leaning on Prince Braevin for support. Together they braved the wind. Xavier stood alone. He widened his stance, folding his arms across his chest in defiance.

The apothecary scuttled away as a blast of wind pursued him. When he disappeared into the crowd, Phoena let him go.

The King proved more stubborn than she expected. The cloak of dark energy remained around her. He held her captive with his arm while his thin hair whipped around his head. When she directed the gust to tear her from his embrace, his magic faltered. King Andressan fell back against the cushioned throne. He snatched at her hand, but the wind pulled her away. His shoulders slumped, but he still held the goblet. She had to keep him from focusing on the potion. Her power needed more time to complete the transformation.

One by one, her regular hairpins pulled free from her head, and then the ribbon came loose. Her long hair fluttered in the breeze, spiralling outward. She stretched out her arms like wings, and her full skirts billowed in the wind as she began to spin.

Then her feet lifted from the floor.

"Ooh!" gasped the crowd.

She floated for a few seconds, captured by the whirlwind. The King's dark cloud reached towards her, bolts of lightning slashing at her brighter sparks. Phoena searched his face for an explanation for the surge in energy. His strength was fading – did he think she needed saving from her own power? She blinked, and the wind ceased. Her hair flopped down to cover her shoulders as she drifted to the floor.

She stood still, her arms by her side – the potion was almost ready. Forty-five seconds more was all she needed. The King stared at her as the silence stretched. Thirty seconds – twenty seconds–

Then he raised the goblet and drained the contents. With a grimace, he threw the cup away from him, and it clattered on the hearth.

CHAPTER 22:
THE
FIRST DANCE

King Andressan held out his arm to Phoena. "Now we will dance," he announced as he dragged himself to his feet.

"Perhaps you should wait for the potion to do its work?" Prince Braevin said.

The King ignored him, and Phoena cautiously approached. He pressed his face into her hair as he wrapped his arm around her waist. "Work your magic," he whispered and then she sensed that his legs were beginning to fail him. She took a deep breath and summoned her strength to keep him upright.

"You heard the King," Princess Ivandelle said. "Let the dance begin."

The spectators opened a path to the centre of the ballroom. The King dictated their pace. Phoena adjusted her grip, using her power to enable him to walk. He sighed. "Thank you. I appreciate this brief reprieve from my torment. How long will it last? Has my sister told you to allow me this dance, or will you humiliate me by having the potion fail?"

The orchestra began playing in earnest when the King limped onto the dance floor. Phoena relaxed – the tune was familiar, and she knew all the steps. For a complete circuit, they had the floor to themselves. King Andressan made no attempt at conversation. When she glanced at his unsmiling face, the arm around her waist tightened. He continued to hold her in a vice-like grip. Phoena bore more and more of his weight, but his steps grew increasingly laboured. His cloud of magic poked and probed her defences, making her task more difficult.

Trusting her power to deal with the King, Phoena partitioned her mind. She watched her feet, counting the dance steps: one, two, three, spin; one, two, three, dip, then reverse... A rustling to the side signalled the arrival of the other dancers. First to join them were Princess Ivandelle and Prince Braevin. Each chose a partner from the Princess's entourage. For a woman in her forties, the Princess was an energetic mover. Other couples crowded onto the dance floor. King Andressan steered Phoena towards the centre of the room. The dancers made way, and then they closed the gap to encircle him at a respectful distance.

Phoena experienced a twinge of envy over the laughing dancers whirling around the room. Even Yiana was giggling as she sailed past with her partner. The Princess grinned each time she went by. Karilion and Nessie were among the crowd of dancers, lost in an enthusiastic argument while they whirled. The dance dragged on, and King Andressan grew even more morose.

Finally, the music reached a crescendo. The orchestra fell silent. The other dancers applauded, bowing to their partners. Phoena tried to curtsey to the King, but his tight embrace made it difficult. He directed her through the crowd, intent on leaving the dance floor. As soon as they were near enough to his throne, he released her. Even with her assistance, he landed heavily on the cushions.

A footman appeared with a low stool, which he placed before the King, close to the monarch's shrivelled left leg. "Sit there," King Andressan said.

Seated on the stool, she adjusted her skirts. From this low position, she sat at right angles to the King. The footman appeared again bearing refreshments. The King selected a glass of wine from the tray. He downed it in one gulp. He chose a second drink, which he passed to Phoena. His hand was shaking – he almost dropped the delicate crystal vessel before she caught it. He reached for another glass and then waved the footman away. She waited for the King to speak, but he remained silent. The dark cloud that hung over him continued to harass her.

The orchestra began to play another tune. Phoena sipped her wine as she watched the dancers assume their new positions. Her foot tapped in time with the music. This dance was more complicated, with a tricky tempo, and the couples swapped partners at every rotation.

Phoena searched for her friends. Yiana was laughing as she moved from one partner to another. Karilion and Nessie were not in the formal group. Eventually, Phoena spotted them dancing off to the side. She rested against the arm of the throne, returning her attention to the central dance formation. Nessie's cousin Meredith passed from her previous partner to join hands with Xavier. The girl smiled and laughed, but there was no reciprocal response. The Marquis spun Meredith around so that he was looking over her head. He stared at Phoena, and she dropped her eyes.

King Andressan finished his second drink, and the footman reappeared. He gave the servant the glass and waved him away. The King groaned as he adjusted his position on the throne, nudging her with his foot. "What do they call you?"

"Phoena, Your Majesty."

"Phoena." His voice was harsh and menacing. She swatted away another attempt by his brooding power to intrude in her mind. He groaned, and his hand brushed against her head. Without warning, he tugged at her hair. A blazing burst of her energy slapped him. Carefully setting down her wineglass, Phoena spun her upper body towards the King. He was nursing his injured fingers.

"How dare you zap me." He sounded like a petulant child.

Phoena bit back a retort. He appeared so frail, more like a hundred years old than forty-five. King Andressan's trembling hand reached for another coil of her hair. Blue light hummed in the air between them as he looped the thick curl around his fingers. Confident that her defences would protect her, she kept still.

"Curious," he murmured. "I can detect no spells, and yet as soon as I reached for your hair, energy appeared from nowhere. Has my sister found a new form of enchantment to enthral me?"

"Your sister knows nothing of this."

"What else have you kept from my sister?"

"I've only met your sister once. I'm a mystery to her."

"Then why did she want me to dance with you?"

"You forget that I wasn't her first choice."

He looked across to where the Princess Royal laughed, surrounded by her followers. The King stretched one twisted leg and grimaced. "Phoena, what did you do to the potion?"

"What makes you think I did anything?"

"The usual numbness is missing. And today, it tasted of honey and aniseed, instead of hemlock and arsenic."

She stared at him. "You knew those poisons were there, and yet you were still prepared to drink it?"

"I've been in pain for more than two decades. I've swallowed worse concoctions in pursuit of relief. On a good day, that potion makes it possible for me to walk upright for a short time."

"And on a bad day?"

He laughed bitterly. "On a bad day, my sister moves closer to her ambition to be queen."

Phoena asked, "Have there been more bad days recently?"

The King held her captive by her hair. "Bad days are inevitable. As my body weakens, the balance of ingredients has to be adjusted." He winced from another spasm of pain. "It takes time to find the new formulation."

"Not every ingredient in that goblet was beneficial."

His reply was harsh. "You're only a child. What do you know about anything?"

She spoke quietly. "I'm trained to detect and neutralise poisons." Phoena pretended the King was one of her Fellowship tutors, quizzing her on her lessons. "That potion contained compounds that had no correlation to pain relief. Two of them were metabolic destabilisers, and another caused painful muscle seizures. You may have experienced temporary pain relief – which ensured you took another dose."

He slumped sideways, closing his eyes as he played with her hair. The dark cloud above his head intensified. "What would you have me do? I cannot endure this pain without medication."

"You won't live very long if you continue to take it," Phoena said. "You ask what you should do – get rid of that apothecary. Find yourself a healer who isn't in the pay of your sister."

His hand jerked, and her defences sent him another jolt for tugging her hair. He glared at her. "Naturally, you recommend yourself for the job."

Phoena sprang to her feet. "No."

Her sudden movement wrenched her hair from his grasp. When she faced him, he still had a few strands trapped in his fingers.

"No? But isn't that what this charade is supposed to achieve? My sister has outdone herself this time. You convince me that you're an ally, and then you take over my torment."

"I don't work for your sister."

"Then who *do* you work for?" His question hung in the air between them.

CHAPTER 23:
A ROYAL ARGUMENT

Phoena looked towards the dancers. Then she glanced in the other direction. A footman stood a discreet distance away, watching to see if the monarch needed anything. This section of the room was growing dimmer as the dark cloud above the King intensified. She called on her defences to increase her protection. In response, the nearby fire shot a few sparks onto the hearth. The footman stepped out of its range. The music and laughter in the room faded.

King Andressan stiffened. Was this evidence that he could see the blue energy forming a domed wall around them? His hand edged towards the jewelled dagger in his belt. Phoena smoothed her skirts and tugged at her gloves. Then she straightened her shoulders before gazing directly into his eyes.

"Have you heard of the Elemental Fellowship?" she asked.

"Of course," he sneered. "Are you telling me the legendary Fellowship is recruiting *children* now?"

"The Fellowship is my family."

King Andressan scanned the room. Another dance ended, and the couples reformed in preparation for the next one. "What does your Fellowship want from me?"

"You're the King. You should be asking what the Fellowship can do for you."

He leaned forward, grinding his teeth as another spasm of pain ripped through his legs. "Tell them to mend my bones," he hissed, clutching her arm. "Or find a way for me to end this misery without handing my sister the Kingdom. If I knew my people would be safe, I would gladly die."

Phoena hesitated before she spoke. "Release my arm." He delayed for almost a minute. When he finally removed his fingers, she rubbed the marks on her skin. She moved slowly. First, she resumed her low position on the stool, and then she swivelled to gaze directly at him. After a long deliberation, she extended one hand towards him. "Keep still."

Blue energy leapt from her fingers. It wrapped itself around one of his legs like a fast-growing vine. He flinched but did not attempt to defend himself. The blue light wrapped around his ankle. It then raced in winding bands all the way to his hip. In four rotations, it traversed the whole leg. The flashing blue band was a brilliant contrast to his black linen pants. Phoena rotated her wrist, and a second spiral wound itself around his other leg. The two strands wrapped about his hips in opposite directions. They twisted and knotted themselves together to form a glowing belt at his waist.

King Andressan pulled at the belt. It stretched as if made from elastic. Then it snapped out of his hand. He winced from the backlash. "What have you done to me?"

"I have given you what you asked for."

The colour drained from his face. He staggered to his feet. Immediately his body crumpled in pain. Phoena caught him as his legs collapsed. Sweat beaded on his forehead, and his hands clawed at her.

King Andressan brought her with him as he toppled backwards onto the throne. He gasped like a fish out of water. "It hasn't worked," he moaned as he clung to her.

The words from one of Ennallya's soothing songs filled Phoena's mind. She began to sing softly. At the same time, her power drew moisture from the air to cool his brow. When his breathing settled, she grew quiet.

"Healing takes time," she said. King Andressan swore, thrusting her from him as his defences wavered. She landed heavily on the floor a short distance from his feet.

"You dare promise me healing!"

Before she could pull herself onto her knees, a firm hand caught her arm. Focused on the King's anguish, Phoena had forgotten to watch for anyone else.

"Is this girl bothering you?" Princess Ivandelle asked, savagely shaking Phoena.

"Leave her alone," King Andressan croaked. "She was only trying to help." He wrenched himself into an upright position. "The potion has worn off."

The Princess released Phoena. The teenager scrambled out of reach, edging closer to the fire. Princess Ivandelle clapped her hands. "I'll summon the apothecary."

The footman hurried over. Before the Princess could give her order, her brother shouted. "No!" Both the Princess and the servant turned towards him. "No," he repeated. King Andressan spoke to his sister. "No more. I'm finished with potions."

The servant took a step back.

"But brother—"

"No buts," he said. "This evening's events have made up my mind. There will be no more treatment."

"But the Council's concerns–"

"They are *my* Council," he muttered. "I'm still their King! Leave me to worry about them." He waved to the footman. "Summon my coach. I'm ready to leave. Get some assistants – you can carry me from here on this wretched throne."

The footman hurried to obey. Princess Ivandelle blinked, an unpleasant smirk replacing her frown. She nodded towards Phoena. There was nothing friendly about the glint in her eyes. "And the girl?"

The Princess's purple mist swirled, seeking to influence him. His darker protection surrounded her spell with a pulsating cloud. The Princess didn't react. Was it possible she couldn't see the King's defences? It was clear that he could see his sister's enchantments. Phoena anticipated swift action. It would bring her joy to see this persuasion spell annihilated. The moment stretched.

Nothing happened.

The King looked at Phoena as if he was seeing her for the first time.

All of her.

She resisted the urge to tug at the bodice of her dress.

He smiled. "What about her?"

The Princess increased her persuasion. "You *will* take her with you."

The teenager squirmed. She was puzzled that her usual defences weren't threatening to remove her from this new danger. She moved closer to the fire.

King Andressan half turned towards his sister. "Why are you so eager for her to leave with me?"

Princess Ivandelle shrugged. "It matters not whether she leaves or stays, brother." She tilted her head and smiled. The persuasion spell increased in power. "I only wish you to be comfortable. The nights are cold..."

With a sharp pop, he demolished the Princess's spell.

"Ivandelle," he said, "Phoena is *not* one of your courtiers." The King's eyes challenged his sister to contradict him. "You know I have refused everyone you've sent to my bedchamber. Why would I take a naive girl?"

"You find the girl *charming*, brother?" The Princess was not giving up without another attempt. Her second spell dove towards him with tenacity. "Now that you've refused the potion, the watches of the night will be painfully long..."

He deflected the enchantment as if it were nothing. "I have long suspected you of being behind the recent mischief at Court. Would you bewitch me into behaving inappropriately towards this girl? You seriously underestimate my power."

Princess Ivandelle laughed. She directed her next spell towards Phoena.

"Stop that," he said wearily, dropping her spell to the floor before it reached Phoena. "It is one thing to toy with the affections of your courtiers, but I cannot allow you to corrupt an innocent child."

The Princess would not concede defeat. She sent another enchantment towards the King. This time, his defences did nothing. The spell wrapped itself around his wrist.

"Open your eyes, brother. This young woman is no child."

His response was quieter. "If I took her with me, her reputation would be ruined."

His sister's smile didn't waver. "Without the potion, you won't live long enough to worry about that. And there's the added reassurance that she has no relatives to challenge you.

Listen to my advice, brother. You've always been soft-hearted, too concerned about doing the right thing. Take her with you and enjoy her company. When you no longer need her, I will find someone to take care of her."

Phoena took a step nearer, her energy building within her. The fire in the hearth behind her popped and hissed. The King kept his eyes locked on his sister, but his hand lifted towards Phoena.

"Stay where you are, girl," he said. There was a flash of dark energy. The glowing band around his wrist disintegrated in a shower of bright sparks. "Leave me to deal with this insult."

A second burst of energy rushed out from the throne in a wide arc. The impulse hit Phoena so hard she stumbled backwards. The Princess didn't budge. She faced the King with her smile still plastered on her face. Her magical defences had been momentarily shredded, but the purple mist was reforming. Princess Ivandelle twitched the fabric of her train. A wild spell went backwards into the crowd. Had her enchantment misfired, or was this a different strategy?

Phoena craned her neck, but she couldn't see where the wayward spell had gone.

King Andressan spoke again. He glowered at his sister. "I'm no fool. I see the trap you've set."

"What trap, brother?"

"Phoena may be an orphan, but she is not without protectors."

"Who would be reckless enough to challenge their King?"

"Look behind you. Karil is pushing his way across the dance floor. I command you to stop using your enchantments against him. News has reached me of your recent visit to *Quenthlaretta College*. You've persuaded him that he's in love with her."

Phoena threw a troubled glance to where Karilion argued with Nessie and Yiana. The familiar purple spell hovered over him. The two girls were tugging on his arms, pulling him in the opposite direction. Most of the dancers stopped to witness the young nobleman's latest embarrassment.

Phoena dropped the privacy barrier that had protected her conversation with the King. The music was loud, but Karilion's voice was louder.

"If I don't do something, the King is going to steal her away."

A momentary lull made Nessie's answer easier to hear. "Have you gone mad? Everyone knows the King is too ill—"

"Shh!" said Yiana. "Are you both trying to get yourselves into trouble?"

The warning came too late. Two members of the Princess's entourage grabbed Karilion, dragging him towards the King. The Princess tapped her toes and nodded.

"Enough," growled King Andressan. He used his power to amplify his voice. The orchestra stopped playing, and everyone turned to face him. "Take Lord Karilion out into the garden and keep him there until he is in his right mind." The Princess's friends hesitated. The King pulled himself painfully to his feet. "Do as I say, or I will banish you from Court."

The men removed Karilion from the room. The youth did not go quietly. Nessie chased after him, muttering about his stupidity. Yiana signalled to Phoena that she would stay with the pair before disappearing from view.

Phoena scanned the crowd. Her godfather followed after Karilion. Other members of the Fellowship were taking up strategic places within the assembly. Her shoulders relaxed, yet the tingling in her arms intensified.

Phoena waited to see if her secret fire would stay hidden.

The orchestra resumed playing, and the King sank back into his seat with a strangled cry. The Princess approached the anguished man and placed her hand on his arm. "You weary yourself," she said. "Let me call the apothecary."

"Get away from me," he muttered. "Why are those servants taking so long?"

"If you won't let me help you, at least allow me to arrange for your departure."

Before he could respond, the Princess waved her hand. Prince Braevin must have been waiting for her signal. He spoke to a nearby nobleman, and came with him towards the throne. Prince Braevin said something to Xavier, who reacted immediately. With a shout, he struck the Prince and thrust the other man aside.

"Oh, dear," Princess Ivandelle said with a smirk. "It seems Xavier has added himself to that list of defenders, brother. You won't find it so easy to get rid of him. At least you don't have to worry about your little friend's reputation. She'll make Xavier a pretty wife, but I don't think she'll last as long as his previous one."

The floor beneath Phoena's feet rumbled. Beside the throne, her forgotten glass toppled over. There were ripples on the surface of the spilled wine as it flowed towards her. The Princess pretended not to notice, but the King's white knuckles clutched the throne. His dark energy consolidated about him.

"The Marquis is under your command," King Andressan said, refusing to look in Xavier's direction. "Phoena has other defenders. She is safe from your meddling."

The Princess smiled sweetly. "I can't see any others. What proof do you have?"

"The evidence is in plain sight," the King said. "Have you noticed the dragon brooch pinned to her dress?" The Princess twisted towards Phoena. The teenager's hand flew to her bodice. "That family crest belongs to Draggo, the Emberite Ambassador. He has two sons, both proven swordsmen. They are also skilled sorcerers. Either one of them would be more than a match for your Marquis. And see that foreign medallion around her neck? The engraving is the designation for a mighty warrior wizard."

"These other suitors – if they exist – are not here, brother."

"But they have been summoned. Can't you feel the vibrations beneath your feet?"

Princess Ivandelle looked down. The shaking intensified until even the overhead candelabra rattled. Some of the women screamed. Several vases toppled over and shattered on the marble floor. Then, as suddenly as it began, the quaking ceased.

"What was that?" Xavier asked when he arrived.

"My brother thinks this girl has wizards and warriors as her defenders," Princess Ivandelle said. "They are coming to save her."

Xavier frowned. He opened his mouth to speak and then changed his mind. As he stared at Phoena, she found herself back in the garden with that black raven watching from the tree. She blinked, and the illusion faded. He smiled and folded his arms.

Prince Braevin appeared. "Save her from what?"

"From anyone who attempts to possess her," the Princess said. "From Xavier, from Karil, and even from the King himself."

CHAPTER 24:
SECRETS REVEALED

Phoena glanced around. The whole assembly drew near to the King.

"Your Majesty," one dignitary said. "What's happening?"

"A little sorcery," King Andressan replied. "This was simply a demonstration of power, nothing more. There is no danger."

"How can you be sure?"

"Look around you," the King said. "Is anyone hurt? If there was any malice, the walls would have tumbled down."

Some of the crowd murmured anxiously.

"There have been troubling revelations this evening," he continued. "Evidence of a conspiracy against the Crown. My sister, the Princess Royal, has aligned with our cousin, Prince Braevin, to take my throne."

"Where is the evidence?" someone cried.

"The Elementary Fellowship has conducted an intensive investigation."

"You risk the stability of your Kingdom on the word of a secretive organisation!" Princess Ivandelle cried. "Who here will admit that they belong to this *Fellowship*?"

The gathered nobility shuffled their feet and remained silent.

"Who here dares to accuse me?" the Princess demanded.

"This girl," King Andressan said, signalling for Phoena to approach him.

"Her!" the Princess sneered. "I don't know what lies–"

As Princess Ivandelle began her verbal attack, her magic cloud intensified. The room chilled, but Phoena's internal temperature soared.

"Silence!" shouted the King.

A blast of magic flashed around the throne. Ivandelle's mouth still moved, but there was no sound. A collective gasp arose from the crowd. Her eyes bulged, and she raised her arms. The spell she sent towards her royal brother fell harmlessly to the floor. Ivandelle grew still, but her purple mist throbbed as the dark cloud gathered around her.

"Is there anyone who will speak in Ivandelle's defence?" King Andressan asked.

"I will speak," Xavier said, stepping forward, "But only to add my voice to her accusers."

A babble of voices responded to his remark.

"What?"

"Surely not?"

"Be quiet! I want to hear what he has to say!"

The Marquis knelt before the throne with his head bowed. He removed his sword and held it towards the monarch with open palms. King Andressan accepted the sword and passed it to Phoena.

"Your Majesty, I plead for your mercy," Xavier continued. "The Princess Royal tricked me into helping her. I'm not alone. Her persuasive deceptions have undermined your subjects' faith in your ability to rule. I am willing to tell the King's Council what I know in return for amnesty."

The Princess's purple mist launched a violent attack at Xavier.

Her accuser threw up his hand, deflecting the spell. It bounced off the ceiling and rebounded into the crowd. A blast of energy leapt from the King, preventing the thwarted curse from reaching the spectators.

Ivandelle stomped her foot and her attention fixed on Phoena again. But before she could raise her arm, the King acted. His magic created a shimmering dome around Ivandelle.

A thick fog obscured what was happening for a few moments. When the cloud faded, Ivandelle stood immobile beside the throne, wrapped in a magical cocoon. Only her eyes were visible.

Xavier pointed towards Ivandelle. "She has been slowly poisoning you, My King. I have interrogated the royal apothecary, and he has confessed to everything."

"Bring the apothecary here!"

"Unfortunately, that's no longer possible, Majesty," Xavier continued. "The man took poison rather than face his angry mistress. I took the liberty of having his body removed."

A servant went to confirm Xavier's claim. Members of the King's Council pushed forward to make their presence known. Nessie's father was one of the first. Lord Westernbrooke was not far behind. Karilion was one of the last noblemen to take his place.

The orchestra quietly played, but the dance floor was empty. The remaining guests clustered in small groups throughout the room. How close they came to the drama depended on which was stronger: curiosity or fear.

The Council members shuffled for a position. King Andressan's magical defences tested each man before permitting their approach. One by one, they bowed to reaffirm their loyalty. In haughty defiance, Princess Ivandelle stood with her head high. Her magic refrained from attacking the King, but her powers hovered above her. Prince Braevin stood beside her with his arms folded. Xavier's father, Duke Urdigo, crossed the room to pull his son to his feet. Together they stood apart from the accused royals.

Momentarily forgotten, Phoena slipped away towards the hearth, with Xavier's heavy sword clutched to her chest. Internal flames blurred Phoena's vision. The warmth of the fire was negligible compared to the raging blaze within.

"You don't look well," Yiana whispered. "Let me have that sword before you drop it."

Phoena surrendered the sword without hesitation.

"Phoena! The metal is red hot!" Yiana cried. Something clattered to the floor at their feet. "Oh, Phoena. It's twisted out of shape. The heat from your hands has ruined Xavier's sword!"

Phoena fanned herself and summoned a moisture-laden breeze. The coals in the grate hissed and dimmed. As her body cooled, she turned to face the hearth, leaning wearily against Yiana. They gazed into the fire, and a blanket of silence settled over them. White-faced, Nessie joined them. With a friend on either side, Phoena remained on her feet.

Magic hummed from around the King's Council until Phoena's head filled with a buzzing sound. It reminded her of a swarm of wild bees she had once encountered. The room wavered, darkness pulsating at the edges of her consciousness. The temptation to remove herself from this place intensified.

Someone touched Phoena on the shoulder. Yiana spun her around to face Cecily. Her frowning godmother's mouth moved, but Phoena heard no words. The teenager closed her eyes, realising too late that it was impossible to re-open them. Her godmother placed a cooling hand on her forehead. Was it the unheard words or the action that robbed the darkness of its potency?

"Concentrate," Cecily's voice whispered inside her head. "There will be no answers for your endless questions if you are not here."

The darkness receded, the room stilled, Phoena's ears opened.

Her godmother leaned closer and nodded. "If you're going to turn the Kingdom upside down, you need to remain to witness the consequences. Always remember – your curiosity will guide your quest."

Phoena asked the first question that came into her head. "Is it true that you were supposed to marry King Andressan? If you had stayed–"

"I wouldn't have found you," Cecily said, shaking her head. "That wasn't the question I expected." She frowned. "If I had stayed, I would have been defenceless against Ivandelle. I didn't want to be her pawn after he died."

"But he didn't–"

"No," Cecily smiled serenely. "All he had left was his Kingdom, and that kept him alive."

Phoena wanted time to meditate on that statement. Instead, she asked another question. "What happens now?"

"That depends on what you've achieved with your meddling." Cecily abruptly turned away.

"Cecily, you must go with the King when he leaves," Phoena said. "He cannot be alone."

Yiana and Nessie both gasped. Cecily froze, slowly facing Phoena with narrow eyes. "Is that a command?"

"Would it make a difference if it was?" Phoena asked.

Her godmother gazed at her for a moment. "I have pledged my life to your service."

"Then serve me by keeping him safe."

"And if I refuse?"

"Ivandelle wins," Phoena said. "Bringing an end to everything you and the Fellowship have strived to achieve. The quest will fail, for I could never serve her."

Phoena retrieved the sword from the floor and straightened it. The reformed blade bore the imprint of her fingerprints but was otherwise perfect.

"Take this to the King. I don't know what he expected me to want with it. I don't trust the Marquis – and I don't want him to have any reason to come looking for me."

CHAPTER 25:
A GARDEN ATTACK

It was past midnight – the King and his escort had departed hours ago. Cecily and Lord Westernbrooke had accompanied him. Most of his noble escort had since returned to the ballroom, but her godparents were still absent. The orchestra played, but there were few dancers. Phoena rested beside the fireplace, with Yiana and Nessie seated alongside.

"He's back," Nessie said, springing to her feet. She waved towards the stairs. "Over here!"

"Who's back?" Yiana asked.

Phoena opened her eyes. Karilion stood alone at the top of the stairs. He was looking straight at her, and he hurried down to the ballroom. But it took him longer to traverse the room because everyone seemed to want to talk to him. Perhaps his popularity was enhanced by the lateness of his return.

"What took you so long?" Nessie demanded, seizing him by the arm and dragging him onto her vacant chair. She dropped onto his lap before he could answer.

"I had to help put the containment spell in place," Karilion said. "Ivandelle is being exiled. The King is also banishing those who refuse to denounce their allegiance to her. They are leaving on a ship tomorrow, for a destination of her choice."

"He's letting her go?" Nessie cried.

"What if she tries to come back?" Yiana asked.

"That's why there's a containment spell. As long as the Kingdom is at peace and the line of succession is secure, Ivandelle won't be able to return."

"The line of succession?" Nessie leapt up, her face red. "Don't tell me Prince Braevin gets to stay!"

"The Prince tried that argument," Karilion said. "He warned that if he left the Kingdom, no-one could prevent Ivandelle from coming back when the King was dead. He asked where the Council expected to find another legitimate heir."

"There are plenty of other royals," Nessie said. "My mother is one of them. I don't see why Prince Braevin thinks that's a problem."

"I'm sorry, Nessie," Yiana said, "but it's a well-known fact that there is more to the succession than that. An heir must prove their eligibility through both the maternal and paternal lines. Your mother's father came from outside the accepted nobility."

"So what will the King do?" Nessie demanded. "It's no secret that Prince Braevin adores the Princess Royal. He'll invite her back as soon as he's on the throne."

Karilion smiled. "Some members of the Council produced lineage documents to prove there's another heir. Satisfied, the Council gave the Prince a choice. He could risk the dungeon or leave on the ship with Ivandelle. He's chosen the ship."

"Who's the heir?" Nessie demanded. "What kind of protection do they have?"

"The Council are going to keep the heir's identity a secret. But don't worry; I'm confident the heir is safe." His smile earned him Nessie's frown.

When Nessie ran out of questions, it was Yiana's turn to extract information from Karilion. "What happened to Xavier?"

"His father paid a huge ransom for his freedom and took him home to Umbryden. That's over three hours by fast coach. I rode with the escort to the county border to make sure. He went in disgrace, a contrite and broken man. Don't expect any trouble from him."

"When can Phoena and I go home?" Yiana asked.

"Lord Westernbrooke asked me to escort you both. Do you want me to summon the coach?"

"Not before I have another dance," Nessie said. "Ivandelle's disgrace didn't break her royal prohibition. It wasn't fair to make me sit out every dance at my mother's ball." She grabbed his hand and dragged him towards the dance floor.

Despite his protest, Karilion soon lost himself to the joy of the dance. Phoena watched them dancing and sighed. "I need fresh air."

"I'll come with you," Yiana said. They walked through the adjoining room. A footman bowed and opened the door that led out into a paved courtyard. After a few steps, Yiana halted. "It's freezing out here. I'll go and get our cloaks."

"I'll wait for you on that bench over there."

Phoena sat shivering in the semi-darkness. Her whole body ached. She considered warming herself, but that required more motivation than she could muster. She yawned and closed her eyes, listening to the nocturnal noises. Somewhere, crickets chirped, and further away, frogs sang to each other. If she turned her head and filtered out the louder sounds, she could hear fast-flowing water. Then above everything else, she detected the soft beating of wings. Some nocturnal creature was enjoying the clear midnight air.

Phoena gazed around her but could find no creature. The water called to her through the darkness. Her eyes lingered on the glowing torch that burned beside a nearby path. Perhaps the walkway down to the unseen river was well lit? She headed into the shadowy garden, her senses alert. Her heart skipped erratically, and one hand held the dragon brooch. Was it futile to hope that shapeshifting Oramis might fly halfway around the world to see her?

Turning a corner, Phoena came to the end of the torches. The river lay at the bottom of the hill, lost somewhere in the darkness. Did the glowing bangle on her wrist provide sufficient light to continue her exploration?

A flutter in the treetops distracted her. There was something different about this sound. Was that a bat or an owl? She scanned the night sky as the sound spiralled around her. Phoena grew dizzy from her effort to catch a glimpse of the creature.

Then the noise ceased. The garden waited in eerie silence – even the shadows were still. The creature must have flown away. Phoena shivered, wrapping her arms around her body and turning towards the house. The gravel beneath her feet crunched as she retraced her steps. The call of the unseen river chased after her on the breeze that raced up the hill.

It was darker ahead. What had happened to the torches? Phoena heard the faintest shuffle and hesitated. "Who's there?"

A piercing screech, like the cry of a carrion bird, shredded the nocturnal peace. Then a flapping creature dove towards Phoena, who protected her eyes with her arms. Something heavy dropped over her head from above, a drapery that was sticky like a spider's web. She wrestled with the heavy covering, and her defences flared. The dense fabric embraced her power, drawing it from her. Her heart stopped for a moment. Long-forgotten memories of imprisonment weakened her hands. When she was a child, something similar had occurred, robbing her of her power.

The hard ground received her without pity.

She lay still, her body racked with pain, while her mind searched for answers. What had happened to her defences? The faintest whisper of blue spark answered her call, too weak to help her. Where had her strength gone? She pushed deeper and deeper into the recesses of her mind.

When she neared the centre of herself, she came against an impenetrable wall. She recoiled, only to be swamped by a flood of memories. Flashes from her past confirmed her worst fears and reawakened her childhood terror. Reliving her three-year-old self's torment paralysed her. The child had fought this magic, not realising that the struggle enhanced its potency. She recoiled from the revelation that she could not save herself.

Breathing shallowly, Phoena pushed back nausea. This time, she was not a helpless child. She still knew who she was. Hadn't fourteen years of servitude proven she was a survivor? She repeated this to herself until her fluttering heart settled to a steadier rhythm. A new hope awakened. Only a few months ago, the One who had gifted her these powers had delivered her. Surely He would do so again.

In control of her emotions once more, Phoena pressed her mind to prayer. She asked for wisdom, patience and endurance...

The memories lost their potency and she turned away from the barrier that separated her from her powers. Slowly, her awareness of the physical world returned.

Phoena remained immobile, sensing the approach of a powerful malignant presence. With a wild flapping, her winged attacker landed beside her.

"How fortunate that I should find you outside alone," a male voice said.

She knew that voice! What was Xavier doing here? Karilion said he had escorted the disgraced Marquis halfway home.

"This has been too easy." Crunching gravel revealed his position at her side. "If I didn't know my gullible father so well, I might think this was a trap." Xavier struck her. Pain ripped through her lower abdomen and her mind retreated from the agony. She refocused on his voice. "The old man believes I'm repentant. I told him I was flying to our mountain retreat to hide."

Xavier scoffed. "Old fool. If he had trusted me with his secrets, I could have avoided Ivandelle's ridiculous schemes. You and I would be allies." He struck her again. "My father said he renounced his membership after the Fellowship stripped you of your powers. His magical inventions were supposed to be used against your enemies. I was a student at the *Academy* when you arrived there as a child." He shook her violently enough to bring tears to her eyes. "If I had known you were there, I would have found a way to free you."

Phoena neither whimpered nor moved. It was harder to remember why she must not fight back. What if the old memories were wrong?

Xavier rolled her onto her back. "But that didn't stop my father's research." He pushed the covering back from her face and retreated to a safer distance. "This cloak is much easier to use than the original box he created. He even left instructions, so there was no risk to my power when I employed the cloak against you."

Phoena slowly focused on his dark form. At first, she thought he was a man again, but then he unfurled the immense wings attached to his shoulders. Had she already known that Xavier was a shapeshifter? She didn't think so. Her captor leaned over her, his hands grasping her shoulders and those outstretched feathers extinguishing the twinkling stars. "I thought I would have to snatch you from the King, but that weakling let you slip through his fingers.

"But none of that matters now," he crowed triumphantly. "You're mine." He said something in an unknown tongue, and the cloak shimmered for a moment. The suffocating, draining sensation ceased, and the fabric felt looser. Phoena concentrated on her shallow breathing, and allowed her mind to drift until she almost forgot the reason for her fear.

Her captor must have waited a long time before he dragged her to her feet. Her legs would not support the weight of her body. Nor would her arms obey a command...

Xavier pulled her to his chest. His face loomed closer. In the dim light, the unnatural gleam in his black eyes froze the blood in her veins. He pressed his lips over her mouth. There was nothing gentle or loving about his kiss.

A different kind of darkness flooded Phoena's mind. Her extremities prickled in warning. What remained of her strength fled as her vision dimmed. She clung to the sound of her heartbeat. Then even that comfort began to falter.

Could he sense the nearness of her death? His lips released her. With a triumphant shriek, her captor launched himself into the air and carried her with him. The magic cloak flapped in the breeze, and the dark inertia in her mind faltered. A lament about the receding landscape awakened in her heart as they rose faster and higher.

Cry out, my soul, cry out.
Let not this moment pass without remark.
Shadowy wings fly over the earth,
Onward and upward without mercy,
Carrying me away from all that I love.
Hope is dying, perhaps it is already too late?

My soul cries out, "Fear not! Fear not!
The All-Sustaining One will not forget His promise.
Darkness will flee at the coming of the light."

The song faded, and a tiny spark flickered at the edges of Phoena's mind. She drew nearer, her senses awakening. It was much colder here. The magic cloak had slipped from Phoena's head but her body was still well-wrapped within her captor's tight embrace. Nothing disturbed the silence except the hypnotic rhythm of Xavier's beating wings.

CHAPTER 26:
WINGED CONTEST

A ferocious roar shredded the night, and darkness fled. Xavier halted in mid-air. The birdman's feathers bristled as he screeched in reply. He flung Phoena from him, transforming into a giant vulture. He rose to face the challenger, while she plummeted towards the distant treetops.

Another roar ripped across the sky. Xavier answered the challenge with a piercing cry. Something larger than her tormentor swooped towards her, but the vulture was faster. He snatched her out of the air with his sharp talons. She dangled from his claws, breathless and dizzy, her heart fluttering. He spiralled away from his mighty foe.

A gust of wind snatched at the loose cloak that had drained her power. A dim veil lifted from her eyes when it fluttered away. A sharp beak and beady eyes were studying her. He adjusted his grip until he held her body with both claws.

As he flew with her dangling beneath him, Xavier launched a powerful magical attack. A mesh of energy swept across the sky. It was distinct against the darker night. The dangerous threads throbbed and pulsed in the air, matched in intensity by a low-pitched hum. Phoena stared at it in wonder.

Her unknown defender veered aside, firing a savage blast of crimson flames towards the spreading enchantment.

Phoena shielded her eyes when the night sky lit up brighter than a dozen suns. When she looked again, all that remained was a vast cloud of sparkling particles. The fire and the spell had annihilated each other. As the cloud drifted away, she caught a glimpse of a familiar silhouette. Xavier was facing a monstrous dragon!

A spark of hope flickered into life. Phoena knew this dragon – Oramis. Her shapeshifting friend had come to liberate her. The captor wheeled and dodged, rising higher and higher, but her would-be rescuer skilfully matched every manoeuvre.

The flaming assault continued. The stench of scorched feathers filled Phoena's nostrils, yet Xavier refused to give up. He fired different spells, each one exquisitely beautiful in its complexity. The dragon dealt with them decisively, but the vulture continued to evade capture.

Only when the dragon came close enough to rake the vulture with his claws did Xavier's strategy change. With a defiant screech, the vulture released her. She dropped like a stone.

Oramis dove towards her. The vulture threw himself at the dragon, plunging those cruel claws into his flank. The two creatures screeched and wrestled above her.

Phoena continued to fall. The distant lights of the grand house appeared beneath her.

The dragon roared again. Somehow, he broke free – one wing tattered – to resume his descent. How badly was he wounded? Her soul screamed in anguish.

Instead of growing, the approaching dragon shrank in size as he came. In his diminutive form, he twisted and writhed to evade the raptor's talons. The battle resembled the futility of a massive lion trying to catch a fragile butterfly.

Was there a chance that Oramis might escape?

The tiny dragon shot towards her like an arrow. With a terrifying hiss, his enemy pursued him. As the distance between hunter and prey narrowed, Xavier resumed his winged-human form. He had triumph written on his face.

The distance between the falling girl and the dragonet shrank. Her friend was now the size of a small cat, his red and black coat glistening in the starlight. Xavier's outstretched hands almost captured the dragon's flailing tail. Oramis crashed into her chest, and she folded her arms around him. Together they continued to fall. A tear trickled down her cheek.

The dragonet blew tiny flames at her face. Phoena frowned. Why was he doing this? The little beast glared at her with red eyes before savagely biting her shoulder. The pain was intense. She screamed, thrusting the tiny dragon from her. His sharp claws pierced her skin and his long serpentine tail wrapped around her waist. The fire intensified and the flames set her bodice alight. Desperately, she beat at the smouldering fabric. Her frantic action sent them into a spin.

Something stirred at the edge of her consciousness.

The shadow of Xavier's wings blocked out the stars. The birdman's hand caught hold of her hair, and he wrenched her towards him. She screamed again. The little dragon leapt to fight her enemy, and Phoena grabbed the tiny creature.

"No!" she cried, desperate to protect her friend. He clawed and hissed at her. Didn't he understand that she was trying to help him? Didn't he remember who she was? What she could do with her powers?

Phoena gasped. Powers? A dizzying confusion of emotions exploded within her, accompanied by intense pain, blinding light and an unbearable heat.

For a moment, the world stilled—

And then she was falling again. Downward she plunged in complete darkness. She was free – Xavier no longer held her captive by her hair.

But her arms were empty. Her freedom had come at a terrible cost. She clawed at the air with her hands, her efforts rewarded with nothing but emptiness.

CHAPTER 27:
AN UNDERGROUND SEARCH

The sound of trickling water greeted Phoena when she awoke. Wet and cold, the miserable teenager raised her head. She was alone in a small cavern, lying in a pool of water. Set in the closest wall was a flaming torch.

Phoena puzzled over this provision. The torch was much larger than those in Nessie's garden, and it burned with a pure orange flame. A flicker of memory eluded her, increasing her self-loathing. Why couldn't she recognise the smoke-free enchantment?

Dragging herself upright, Phoena studied her surroundings. Her supernatural powers may have left her, but she still had work to do. Xavier must not win.

Reflected light danced within a crystal-clear waterfall that dropped from a higher ledge. The cascade was no wider than Phoena's waist. It collected in the shallow pool in which she lay. Cautiously, she extended her hand. The tingling liquid awoke her thirst, and she drank deeply. Refreshed, she scrambled to her knees.

The top of the waterfall was too far above her, and brooding darkness concealed the cavern roof. Could she climb up to that small ledge and follow the water back to its source? She searched the rock wall, seeking a handhold. After a struggle, she conceded the climb was impossible.

Phoena crossed the cave towards the torch. As she approached, strange carvings on the wall became visible. She stared at them, wondering if the one who had provided the torch had left a message in the marks.

If only she could read them?

Phoena gasped.

Was it her imagination, or was the ornament hanging around her neck vibrating? The medallion that Baraapa had given her was definitely growing hotter and heavier.

Studying the medallion awoke certainty. The engravings were similar to the wall markings. She rubbed the metal object, and a humming sound tickled her ears. It seemed to be coming from the ornament. She drew it closer. As she concentrated, the sound grew louder and deeper, resonating through her body.

Was it her imagination, or was there an answering vibration coming from the wall? With the medallion in her hand, she pressed her other palm on the rock. Both the metal ornament and the wall thrummed in unison as the sound intensified. Even the ground beneath her feet quaked.

Phoena took a deep breath. With great care, she placed a fingertip at the top of the design and began to trace the deep grooves.

The rock carving felt smooth against her skin. She concentrated on her task while her heart cried out with an intense longing to understand the writing. Suddenly, the vibrating stopped. Phoena stepped back. The marks had become an inscription she could read:

Seek the light

Trust the stream

Watch for me

Baraapa is near

What was the explanation for this? First, Oramis had appeared in the sky, and now Baraapa had left her a message deep underground. How had they known of her need?

She scanned her surroundings. The water exited the pool as a bubbling stream which ran away through a narrow tunnel. An orange glimmer in the darkness suggested there was another torch in that direction.

Gathering her damp skirts to her knees, Phoena hurried into the tunnel. The same inscription was on the wall beside the next torch. She ran on, with the stream always beside her. When she found the same message beside a third torch, she smiled and increased her pace.

Baraapa's power had an earth-affinity, and he was an expert with technology. If anyone could provide an easy way for her to journey deep underground, it would be him. By the time she found the sixth torch, she was confident of her assessment. At first, the stream had flowed through a series of natural caverns. But now, the tunnel was a comfortable height and width, a smooth footpath carved through solid rock.

At the seventh torch, she came to a divided path. The stream split into two watercourses around a plinth of granite that barred the way. There were torches in both passageways. She hesitated. Two illuminated options suggested either road would bring her to the surface. But which path would deliver her more speedily?

Taking a deep breath, she chose the left tunnel. She went as far as the next torch and shouted into the darkness. "I'm here! Where are you?" Her echoing voice was the only reply. Phoena retraced her steps and repeated the process in the other tunnel. She waited, her heartbeat pounding in her ears.

The echo faded. She closed her eyes. How was she to make this decision? She walked back to where the path divided.

Then out of the darkness came another voice, faint but distinct. "We're here!"

H-eeeeerrrr-yah! sang the echo.

The voice called again. "Stay where you are."

Staaaaaay where yooooou aaarrrrrrre.

Phoena sat down beside the granite plinth, wrapping her arms around her legs. As she waited, she puzzled over this new development. That was Nessie's voice. How did her blue-haired friend get down here?

CHAPTER 28:
REGENERATING FIRE

Silently, Phoena watched Baraapa take a flint from the bag at his waist. The foreign nobleman knelt beside the enormous pile of timber he had with him, preparing to light a fire. When the sparks ignited his kindling, Baraapa fed the flames with larger sticks. He continued until the blaze could look after itself. Then he rocked back on his heels and looked at her across the flickering flames.

There was something in his gaze that echoed the cold misery in her soul.

Spreading the skirts of her ruined ball gown around her, Phoena sat as close to the fire as she dared. So far, she had avoided any conversation with the other members of their small group. Nessie, Yiana and Karilion had remained apart, whispering together in the shadows. That was about to change.

Nessie's voice carried as they approached. "I still want to know why he didn't ask her to light the fire."

"Not now," Karilion said. "We've agreed to let Yiana ask the questions."

With a sigh, Phoena wrapped her arms around her knees and waited for the inquisition to begin.

"What happened to you?" Yiana asked.

Phoena shivered, readjusting her skirts. The silence lengthened.

"That wet dress looks heavy and uncomfortable," Karilion said. "Why don't you let the girls help you out of it?"

Shaking her head, Phoena focused her attention back on the flames. She did not want to be wearing only her petticoats should further trouble befall her.

"Why doesn't she–" Nessie began, and Karilion elbowed her in the ribs.

Phoena spoke her first words. "What are you doing down here?"

All eyes stared in her direction.

"We were worried about you," Yiana said. "You weren't in the garden when I stepped out with your cloak. I asked the footman, but he didn't know where you were. I went inside to ask–"

"Ask!" Nessie cried. "Yiana, you hauled Karil from the dance floor. There was no way I was going to let you steal him–"

"Nessie made such a fuss, the orchestra stopped playing," Karilion said. He did not attempt to hide his delight. "Everyone came outside to see what she would do next."

"They got more than they bargained for," Nessie said. "When the sky fighting started, magical sparks fell like rain and the footmen ran around putting out fires. Nobody knew where the creatures had come from. Of course, I wanted the dragon to win."

"I *knew* the dragon was Oramis," Karilion said.

"But you didn't know who the vulture was. You scoffed when Yiana said it must be Xavier."

Karilion shrugged. "But I was the first to realise the vulture had Phoena."

"We agreed something terrible had happened to you," Yiana said. "The only magic was coming from the vulture and the dragon."

Another uncomfortable silence fell upon the group. Phoena puzzled over their words – wasn't a powerful vulture and a dragon magic enough?

"Which reminds me," Nessie huffed at Yiana. "I knew you could detect spells, but you never told me you could *see* magic."

Karilion snorted. "There's a lot of things people don't tell *you*." The blue-haired girl leaned across Phoena to punch him. He caught hold of Nessie's hand.

Baraapa spoke for the first time. "Children, behave." He threw another branch on the fire, and sparks flew into the air. Karilion and Nessie stopped wrestling and sat still. Until now, the warrior giant had ignored their bickering.

The group sat in a tight circle around the fire. Karilion sat between Baraapa and Phoena, while Nessie held tightly to Phoena's arm. Yiana sat beside Nessie with her eyes fixed on Baraapa. There was a sizeable gap between the young woman and the foreign warrior. He wore only his waistcoat and long baggy pants. His feet were bare, and his bulging muscles glistened with a coppery hue in the firelight.

"Who are you calling a child?" Karilion complained to Baraapa. "You're three months younger than me, and Nessie's at *least* a year older than either of us."

"Then the pair of you should act your age," Baraapa said. "Lady Firebird asked you to explain your presence here. Get on with your story."

"That's what I was doing," Nessie said, "before my *younger* cousin interrupted me." She poked her tongue out at Karilion, but then she swung towards Phoena. "Lady Firebird? You didn't tell Yiana and I you had a title."

"Not now, Nessie," Yiana said, shaking her head. "You begged us to let you tell Phoena what happened."

"Oh, all right. Stop nagging, but when this is over Lady Firebird and I are going to have a serious talk about what other secrets she's keeping from me." Nessie played with the ruffles on her sleeves and then began again. "We were watching the battle. When the vulture dropped you, Yiana and I screamed. Karil insisted there was no need to worry. He said your defences would activate at any minute. But you kept falling. Then Karil lost it. He shouted at Oramis to do something."

"He heard me," Karilion muttered. "You both cheered when the dragon shrank and evaded capture."

"We didn't expect Oramis to make matters worse."

"Don't say that!" Phoena cried. A tear trickled down her cheek.

"He'll turn up," Karilion said. He attempted to hug Phoena, but Nessie batted his arms away.

"She doesn't need *you*," Nessie hissed.

"That's where you're wrong," Karilion grumbled. "Phoena needs each of us. That's what the legend says. We're a team. Which means Oramis must have survived. It takes more than a feathered traitor to put an end to one of Phoena's champions."

"Get on with your tale," Baraapa said.

"At that point, we all thought Phoena and Oramis were going to perish," Yiana said. "It was awful."

"I couldn't think of a single spell that would help," Karilion admitted.

"Karil cursed when the vulture shapeshifted, and he saw who your enemy was," Nessie said.

Karilion glowered at Nessie. "Nobody knew Xavier could shapeshift."

"He's a lot more powerful than he let anyone know," Yiana concluded.

The group fell silent.

"That's a similarity he shares with each of you," Baraapa said. "If this shapeshifter had known the extent of your powers, he would have dealt with each of you first – before he attacked Phoena."

"You still haven't explained how you came to be here, Baraapa," Karilion said.

"Later," Baraapa replied. "I want to hear your side of the story. There are lessons to learn. We need to be more prepared for the next time."

"You don't think he'll try again?" Nessie cried, pulling Phoena into a tight embrace.

Karilion frowned at Baraapa. "Why do you want to hear what happened? With Oramis wounded and Xavier claiming victory, Phoena's death seemed imminent – and then whoosh! All three of them were gone. I realised what had happened. She's done this before when confronted with danger, transporting herself somewhere safe. All I had to do was find an underground river–"

"You couldn't have found it without me!" Nessie cried.

"We couldn't have done it without Yiana either," Karilion retaliated. "You said there were four nearby rivers. I was ready to search them all, but Yiana stopped me. After listening to her, I knew what to do next."

"Well, I still don't understand," grumbled Nessie. "What was so important about *her* ideas?" Nessie turned to Yiana. "Tell Phoena what you said to Karil and see if *she* can work out what you meant."

"I asked Karil two questions," Yiana said, keeping her eyes on Phoena. "First, I wanted to know how Oramis came to be here. And then I wanted to know what the remaining champion—"

"Baraapa," Karilion said. "His name is Baraapa."

"I wanted to know what *Baraapa's* special skills were."

"What did you tell her?" Baraapa asked, leaning forward.

Karilion laughed. "Strength and wisdom – and a curiosity that's annoying. You're a persistent plodder. If you start something, you won't stop until you get what you want. But Phoena is an exception – you'll have to work a lot harder to win her heart."

Nessie frowned, glancing from Karilion to Phoena, before staring into the fire.

"You forget that Baraapa has earth-affinity, and he's creative – Baraapa's good at making things," Phoena said. "He's always helpful."

"Thank you, My Lady," Baraapa said, smiling across the fire towards her. The orange-haired giant winked at Karilion. It was Karilion's turn to frown.

"That's what I deduced," Yiana said. "I agree with Baraapa – the whole team had to come together. Karil and Nessie were already here. That meant the summons for Oramis and Baraapa would need a speedy response. It made sense that the champion who could fly would carry the other one."

The quiet warrior affirmed her deduction with a nod.

"Tonight I realised why you keep Yiana around, Nessie," Karilion said. "She has enough brains for both of you."

Nessie poked Yiana. "Stop trying to impress everyone with your 'deducing'. Nobody's going to believe you worked that out."

Yiana's cheeks reddened. "While you were flirting with Karil—"

"I was not!"

"Shh!" Yiana snapped. "While Phoena was meeting the King, Lady Cecily and I had an informative conversation. She wanted to prepare me in case Phoena disappeared. On previous occasions, Phoena was only able to come back when her champions were with her. She only had three then, and now she has more. Lady Cecily suggested all the champions had to be together."

"So Oramis had to be with her when she disappeared," Karilion said. "That explains the cute baby dragon act – he's always trying to gain an advantage over the rest of us."

"Baraapa worked underground," Yiana said. "I knew he must be responsible for the earthquake in the ballroom. He made the tunnels and set the torches to help Phoena find her way."

"Karil transported us below after I located the river that had the most caverns," Nessie said. "It was right below my family estate. I told Yiana to remain behind, but she insisted on coming."

"I'm glad Yiana came with you," Baraapa said. "Without her, the pair of you would still be in the first cave, arguing at the top of your voices. I was on my way to silence you when I heard Yiana's voice of reason. You were foolish not to heed her warning. She was right – you had no way of knowing who – or what – might be listening."

"It didn't matter how much noise we made," Nessie said, her voice rising. "Xavier isn't down here!" Then she looked at the faces of the others. "He isn't, is he?"

"Where do you think he went?" Baraapa asked. The cavern quaked at his thundering voice.

"Don't worry, Nessie," said Karilion, frowning at Baraapa. "Oramis is down here too. He's making sure Xavier doesn't find us. At any minute, he'll make a dramatic entrance. He never misses an opportunity to declare himself the great hero."

"He's wounded," Phoena said, struggling to her feet. "We should be looking for him."

"Nonsense!" Karilion said. "If there's one thing I've learned about Oramis, he's difficult to eliminate. It will take more than your feathered fiend to put him out of the picture."

"I'm so glad to receive your vote of confidence," a voice said from the gloom.

Oramis limped into the circle of light. Phoena ran to meet him. He held up his hand to slow her approach. "Careful, My Lady. I'm not at my best."

Battered and bruised, with one eyelid swollen shut, he was almost unrecognisable. Strips from his shredded black shirt bound his torso, the improvised bandages moist. Blood trickled down his leg from an open wound.

"You're bleeding," Phoena said, not hiding her tears. "Oh, Oramis. We have to get help."

"It's nothing," he said, but then he stumbled. In an instant, she caught him. Oramis rested against her as she helped him into the circle. "Get me closer to the fire." When they reached the fire, he sighed. "My Lady, I'm grateful to see you uninjured." Before she could reply, he kissed her forehead.

"Enough of that," Karilion said, pulling Phoena away. "Here's your fire," he said to Oramis. "We'll wait for you to regenerate before you tell us your story."

Oramis stared into the flames. Something incomprehensible flashed across his face – a mixture of grief and disappointment? He glanced across the fire to Baraapa. "Thank you, friend, for your provision."

His transformation into a tiny dragon was instantaneous. As he dove into the fire, Nessie screamed. Karilion scoffed as his cousin covered her face with her hands. Phoena settled before the fire and studied the flames. An uneasy stillness fell on the group.

"I can't sit here doing nothing," Karilion said after half an hour. "Nessie, come and show me where the fish are hiding. I'm sure there are big ones where the water is deeper. We'll catch breakfast."

The pair went into one of the downstream tunnels and their bickering voices faded. Yiana edged closer to Baraapa. She whispered to the warrior, and he nodded. Phoena strained to hear what they said.

"How long will this regeneration take?"

"As long as necessary," Baraapa replied, his voice soft like a pebble rolling downhill. "It would be sooner if there were magic fuelling the flames, but until Lady Firebird remembers who she is, my fire will have to do."

Yiana thought about that for a long time and then she yawned.

Baraapa stretched and rose to his feet. "Get some rest while you wait."

"What are you going to do?" Yiana asked, scrambling to her feet. She threw a glance towards Phoena.

"There's a tunnel to the surface for me to prepare."

"I'll come with you," Yiana said. "You can answer more of my questions."

Baraapa laughed. "Your company would be welcome." Together they went towards the source of the stream.

Finally, Phoena was alone. She stretched her aching limbs and circled the fire as she pondered her situation. Her companions hadn't asked about her experience. Nor had they pressed her to explain why her powers had abandoned her. She returned to her original place and sat down again. Her breath caught in her chest when the fire crackled, but nothing happened. She searched through her returning memories. There must be a hint that would reawaken the fire alluded to by Baraapa. Her heart was tender, her self-confidence crushed.

The coals in the fire stirred, sending a shower of sparks high into the air. Phoena followed them with her eyes. When they faded, she looked back to the flames. Oramis, in his human form, stood before her. The scratches on his still-bruised face had crusted over. His black outfit was once more immaculate. The rips and tears were gone – more evidence of his magic.

He grinned. "The fire has done enough," he said. Yet he clutched his wounded side as he lowered himself to the ground between Phoena and the fire. "Don't look so worried. I'm still drawing heat from the coals. Everything is going to plan. By the time the others return, I will be able to walk unaided."

"What happened to Xavier?" Phoena asked.

"Is Xavier your birdman?" Oramis asked. "My Lady, you should be more careful in your choice of suitors." He waggled his finger at her. "When I saw him last, he was in his human form, wandering in the dark. I caved in some of Baraapa's tunnels. For now, he's stuck in a distant maze without an exit. It will take him time to work out how to escape."

"You didn't kill him?"

"Is that what you expected, My Lady? I had to keep my distance – he's a skilful sorcerer. He knew my injuries were severe, and I'm sure he had plenty left in his arsenal that could destroy me. It was more important to survive and return to you."

"He didn't fight fair. You would have defeated him easily if he hadn't dropped me."

"He took a calculated risk. Perhaps I would have done the same were our roles reversed." Oramis shrugged. "You were only valuable to him if he was winning."

"Why did you stop attacking him? You had the advantage."

He put his hand on his chest, but the laughter remained in his voice. "I'm hurt that you can ask me that. Victory would have been meaningless if you perished."

"I thought he was going to kill you."

"For your sake, I would have made that sacrifice," he said. "But your fears brought you unnecessary pain. I knew all I had to do was re-awaken your powers, and then you could save us both."

"Is that why you attacked me? I thought you were angry with me."

"For that, I am sorry, dear Lady," Oramis said. He grew thoughtful. "I can see the scratches on your skin. I didn't mean to draw blood. Will you permit me to heal you?"

Phoena stared at him, searching her fragmented memories. Despite failing to find any clue behind this offer, she nodded. Oramis transformed into the tiny red-and-black dragonet. He blew flames at the injuries on her neck and arms. She felt heat and pain in equal measure. He hovered in front of her nose, and her fingers touched the delicate, restored wings. There was no remaining sign that the battle had almost destroyed him. She sighed, and her tears resumed.

The dragonet chirped, and then a puff of smoke escaped his nostrils. That was her only warning before his flames blasted her full in the face. Phoena's scream ripped her apart. She lashed out with her arms, sweeping the air where her attacker must be, but a river of tears blinded her. The attack was relentless. Only when she was a weeping mess on the cavern floor did he cease. The heat in her eyes and the anguish lingered long after the attack ended.

When her vision cleared, the unrepentant dragon-lord sat beside her in human form. He studied her and then he reached for her hand. She recoiled, slapping his hand away. Sparks leapt from her fingers towards him. She looked down in surprise. "I thought my power had left me!"

He grinned as he leaned sideways, wrapping her in a tight embrace. "It's only fair that you reward me for my efforts." The sparks at her fingertips turned into flames, and her whole body radiated heat. He sighed, closing his eyes.

Phoena sensed the power flowing from her as the dragon lord grew hotter. A flash of memory stilled her heart. What if Oramis was no different to Xavier?

Whoosh! A brilliant light filled the whole cavern. The flames that burst from within her smashed Oramis against the cavern wall. He sprawled on the ground where he landed. Smoke wafted upward from his clothes. When he sat up, the injuries to his face were gone.

"That was more effective than I hoped for," the blond nobleman said, leaping to his feet. "My Lady, your passion ignites a fire in my heart."

Speechless, Phoena glared at him.

His exultation didn't diminish as he approached her. He dropped to one knee before her and took her hand. "There's a lot more that I could say, but the others are returning."

Phoena had heard nothing. She glanced behind her – a shimmering barrier spread across the tunnel entrance. She looked at Oramis in alarm, and he dismissed her concern. "The others didn't need to hear you scream, My Lady."

Her temper flared, and she demolished his enchantment with a gesture. He shuffled to her side as he held up his hand. "Shh! There will be time to discuss this later," he whispered. "Now, I want to enjoy Karilion's reaction when he sees me alone with you."

"What!"

Oramis laughed louder. "He has no scruples about flirting with every female who crosses his path, but he's jealous around you. I've almost convinced him you like me more than him."

" *Why* – would I – *like* – *you?*"

He blew her a kiss. "Because I wake the fire in you."

Before she could reply, Karilion shouted, "Oi! Don't believe anything that devious spy tells you." The dark-haired nobleman strode to join them, with Nessie on his heels.

"Didn't I tell you, dear cousin," Karilion said to Nessie, "that Oramis would try to steal an advantage in our absence?"

Phoena stood to greet them and Oramis sprang to his feet beside her.

Karilion brandished a pair of massive fish at his rival. "Here, take these," he said to Oramis. "You're such an expert with fire – you can oversee the cooking."

Oramis accepted the fish with a grin. They were already gutted and ready for the flames. He made a grand display of reaching into the fire to place them on the coals.

"Show off," Karilion muttered before turning to Phoena. "Let me wash the fishy smell from my hands, My Lady, and I will convince you of my devotion."

"You will do no such thing," Nessie said. She stood with her hands on her hips. "If either of you lay a finger on Phoena, I'll drown the pair of you."

Both men looked at diminutive Nessie. Karilion grinned and put his hands behind him. Oramis bowed to her and turned his back to kneel by the fire, chuckling as he flipped the fish over.

"Well said, Nessie," Baraapa said, emerging from the shadows with Yiana at his side. "How fortunate that I renounced my claim on our Lady's affections long ago. That will keep me safe from your terrible threat."

Karilion and Oramis laughed, and Baraapa matched their smiles.

Nessie's face flushed. She pointed to the nearby stream, and the surface of the water began to stir.

"Enough!" Phoena said. The whole cavern trembled as that single command echoed across the confined space. One by one, the others swung towards her and stared.

"At last," Baraapa said, and he bowed before her. "Welcome back, My Lady."

"No more of that, either," she muttered. "I haven't had time to test anything."

Baraapa rose to his feet and backed away in haste.

Phoena lifted her arm. "Air." A strong wind circled the cavern, extinguishing all the torches.

The fire flickered. Phoena stretched out her hand. "I need light." A golden sun appeared on her palm. With a swish of her fingers, it whooshed towards the ceiling of the cave, increasing in size and intensity. The cavern became as bright as a glorious summer's day.

"Thank you, Nessie, for defending my honour, but there is no need for any concern." Phoena looked at the stream. "Water." A mighty wave rose above the watercourse. It raced off into the distance, roaring as it went. She turned to Oramis. A dark rain cloud appeared over his head.

"Don't," he said. "If you rain on me, you'll ruin your breakfast."

Phoena smiled. "Your concern for my breakfast is touching." She stepped to the side. "Earth." A slab of black granite emerged from the cavern floor at her feet.

With a small rumble, six stone platters appeared on the makeshift table.

The fish flew from the flames and divided themselves among the platters. Finely-wrought silverware completed her provision.

Baraapa applauded.

Karilion moved behind Nessie. "Protect me, dear cousin, from the fury of our leader. I'm going to need your water enchantment protections, for the next thing she will say is 'fire'."

Phoena laughed. Tiny blue flames appeared at her fingertips. "You don't have to fear my fire. I will reserve my fury for my enemies."

At her invitation, the others assembled around her table. Phoena ate little, despite her ravenous hunger. When her vision finally cleared, the other plates were empty. Oramis had seated himself opposite. He winked at her before stealing her plate. Karilion snarled in protest, but she silenced him with a glance. He scrambled to his feet.

"It's time we took you home," Karilion said, offering Phoena his arm. "Will I transport you to Sumnarscote now?"

"You'll only get her lost," Nessie snapped.

"Baraapa can give me the coordinates—"

"Why do you expect Baraapa to be of any help?" Nessie asked. "He's not a human compass."

Yiana leapt to the warrior's defence. "Baraapa's already shown me which direction Sumnarscote is from here. He uses the earth's magnetic field to find his way underground."

"Karilion can take us to my garden," Nessie said.

"I'm sure My Lady would rather fly home with me," Oramis said, licking the last of the fish from his fingers.

Phoena ended the argument. "We will travel together. It's time we started working as a united team. Baraapa has already opened the way to the surface for us."

It took a few minutes to consign the evidence of their meal to the fire. The plates became dust beneath their feet. Yiana rinsed the silverware in the river. Phoena told her to keep the shiny implements as the first instalment towards her dowry, and they disappeared into Yiana's pockets. The table remained for a future rendezvous.

The golden sun glided ahead of them as Baraapa led them steadily upwards through a maze of tunnels. Yiana walked beside him, engaging him in earnest conversation about the geological features that they passed. Phoena slowed her pace, smiling when Yiana showed him the bracelet on her arm.

But that brought her closer to the bickering pair behind her, and she grimaced. Would those cousins ever stop fighting?

A flurry of wings announced the return of Oramis in his tinier dragon form. He circled the golden orb three times, then swooped down towards her. He ruffled her hair with his talons and flicked her nose with his tail when she shooed him away with her hand. Undeterred, the dragon lord hovered in her face for a moment and chirped at her.

"What's he saying?" Karilion asked. "Lady Firebird, you should order him not to talk to you in dragonish."

"There's no such thing as dragonish," Nessie scoffed. "I think it's endearing the way he blows smoke rings at her face and tries to perch on her shoulder. I'd love to have a pet dragon."

"I'm not a pet," Oramis said, transforming into his human form beside Phoena. He was walking backwards. "A dragon wouldn't last long with you, Nessie. One inconvenient spark and you'd extinguish his fervour with your watery spells. If you're going to aspire to a mythical creature for a pet, a mermaid would be better."

"There's no such th–" Nessie began.

"Let's not get into a long debate about mythical creatures," Phoena said, taking Oramis by the arm and spinning him around to face forward. "Nessie, please be quiet for a moment. You're distracting Oramis, and he insisted he had something important to report."

Oramis kept in step with her as they walked. "Thank you, My Lady. I hope you are satisfied with the endeavours of your humble servant."

"You, humble," Karilion muttered.

Phoena held up her hand as a warning. "Be quiet. From now on, nobody has permission to speak. Oramis, get on with your report."

"There's no sign that Xavier has been able to follow us," Oramis said. "And I can confirm Baraapa's assurance that we are less than twenty minutes' walk from the surface."

"Let's hurry then. I'm eager to feel the sun on my face," Phoena said.

The group increased their pace but nobody dared to speak. Phoena enjoyed the brief respite, turning her thoughts inward to consider what might await her above ground. The tunnel lightened as the gradient increased. The tunnel curved, concealing their view of the way ahead.

Phoena continually adjusted the intensity of her small sun as they walked onward.

A few paces ahead of them, an opening appeared in the rock. Phoena's heart skipped when Baraapa stopped and turned to face her. He gestured to the entrance and bowed low before her. Then he raised his head and he smiled. "Permission to speak, My Lady? May I suggest that you send Oramis to scout out the land."

Oramis didn't wait for her permission, transforming into the dragonet and swooping past Baraapa. He disappeared through the opening.

Phoena waved her hand and her orb of light faded until it disappeared. Oramis was back before her eyes adjusted. He stood beside Baraapa and waited for her to notice him before he also bowed low.

"The way ahead is clear, My Lady. Your servant awaits your further instruction."

Phoena smiled and stepped forward, and the group parted to make way for her. The tunnel mouth emerged between large boulders, high on the side of a mountain. The six adventurers stepped into the open as the real sun rose above the horizon. Phoena inhaled deeply, her heart rejoicing at the dawning of a new day. The words from an ancient song sprang into her mind.

Mythianwtha araamiline...

Phoena sighed, and the modern translation burst from her mouth: "Awake, my soul and greet this new day..."

When the song came to an end, her companions were staring at her in awe.

"I've never heard that song sung like that," Nessie whispered, brushing away a tear.

Yiana hurried to Nessie's side and hugged her friend. "Even the old things are new when you open your heart to believe."

Phoena gazed out upon the land before her. A thin frost sparkled on the ground. Far below, Nessie's estate bathed in the early morning's glory. The King's Citadel shone in the middle distance.

As they lingered there, lost to their own thoughts, the early morning shadows fled. The world seemed vibrant and renewed.

A pair of swallows spiralled overhead, the first sign that spring was on its way.

THE END
OF BOOK 2

CHARACTER LIST

Phoena, Miss Ashton – student at *Quenthlaretta College*

Cecily, Lady de Montnoir – Phoena's godmother, member of the Elementary Fellowship

Lady Ennallya – member of the Elementary Fellowship, healer, mystic

Elemental Fellowship – secret organisation dedicated to protecting the legendary Elemental Champion

Lord Westernbrooke aka Westy – Phoena's godfather, member of the Elementary Fellowship and the King's Council

Nessandra, Lady Cascade, aka **Nessie** – student at *Quenthlaretta College*, Karilion's cousin

Yiana, Lady Yianothalis – student at *Quenthlaretta College,* Nessie's closest friend

Paulo, Lord Yianothalis – Yiana's father, member of the King's Council

Lady Meredith – student at *Quenthlaretta College,* Nessie's cousin

Mrs Viola Hammersley –*Quenthlaretta College* principal

Madame Devinette – philosophy teacher at *Quenthlaretta College*

Master Fitzgibbons – heraldry Master at *Quenthlaretta College*

Daisy – maid at *Quenthlaretta College*

Princess Ivandelle aka the Princess Royal – sister to the King, second in line to the throne

Urdigo, Duke of Umbryden – Xavier's father, Member of the King's Council

Lady Avarina – Princess Ivandelle's lady-in-waiting, sister to Hillarina

Lady Cassandee – Princess Ivandelle's lady-in-waiting

Lady Hillarina – Princess Ivandelle's lady-in-waiting, sister to Avarina

Xavier, Marquis of Umbryden – Duke Urdigo's son, member of the King's Council, Princess Ivandelle's supporter

Prince Braevin – cousin of King Andressan and Princess Ivandelle, third in line to the throne

Karilion, Lord of Hemington, aka Karil – Phoena's champion, Nessie's cousin, member of the King's Council

King Andressan – Ivandelle's brother, Braevin's cousin, Lord of the Western Empire, Commander of the Five Seas

Baraapa, Viscount of Larimore – Phoena's champion

Oramis, Lord of Oramis – Phoena's champion, son of Draggo of Oramis

Draggo Oramis, Emberite Ambassador – father of Lord Oramis

Locations:
Sumnarscote – Lady Cecily's home
Quenthlaretta College
King's Citadel – King Andressan's city, centre for the King's Council

FANTASY RIVER SERIES

PHOENA'S QUEST 1: FIRST SPARK

The quest selects its unlikely champions: an orphaned servant girl, and three privileged young noblemen trying to win a wager. The darkness stirs. Is there time to save Phoena from the awakening magic? There's a dragon in the back garden...

PHOENA'S QUEST 3: THIRD FIRE (2022)

Five champions have been selected to accompany Phoena on her quest. An ancient prophecy, a political storm, and an unexpected threat from the sea draws Phoena and her friends into a contest that will come at a great cost.

OTHER BOOKS

River Wild Romantic Suspense Series

Available at www.chrissygarwood.com

Book 1 (2019) White Rose of Promise

Book 2 (2019) When Promises Are Broken

Book 3 (2020) When Freedom is Promised

Book 4 (2020) Which Promise This Time?

Book 5 (2021) When Promises Are Forever

Book 6 (2021) Waiting For A Promise

Book 7 (2022) Who Pays The Piper?

At first glance, Phoena's story has little in common with my other books. Phoena's world is one where magic and fantasy are an accepted part of everyday life, and the *River Wild* stories are set in contemporary Australia.

But Phoena's world began as a dream sequence in the first *River Wild Romantic Suspense Novel: White Rose of Promise*. I have included an excerpt from that story here:

page 57 (*White Rose of Promise,* paperback edition, 2019)

Ria was certain she was dreaming. All around her, swirling rainbows of light flashed in harmony with waves of pain. This breaking surf was drawing her down into a blue whirlpool. She tried to open her eyes, and the world exploded in a galaxy of iridescent stars. A strange darkness enveloped her like a raging torrent, then the pain faded to a distant memory.

Nothing remained but the heavy darkness. Now she floated, a soothing river bearing her gently towards a distant light. The glimmer turned into a glow. This grew until it burned like holy fire and consumed everything else. Her heart responded to the light, and she knew she was in the presence of God. Now on her feet, she was surrounded by crystal purity, overcome by a peace beyond description.

The fantasy river makes an appearance in each of the stories, which also include dreams and visions, prophesy and wondrous signs. Each of the books in the *River Wild Romantic Suspense series* feature the river as an important element that leads to character transformation.

ACKNOWLEDGEMENTS

This series could not have been written without the support and encouragement of many people.

Firstly, I am grateful to God for inspiring me, for giving me the time and the persistence to bring this story into life.

My writing adventure has not been a solitary one. God provided me with a supportive team - determined to ask the right questions to keep me moving forward. Thanks to Naomi McGlone, Katisha & Trish O'May, Ray Woodrow, Danielle Campbell, Eva Bitterova, Belinda McGuire, Tim Berry, and Donna Bullen for your help with *PHOENA'S QUEST*. I am thankful to Donita Bundy, for the stunning cover.

A special thanks to Belinda Pollard, publishing mentor and editor, for taking me under her wing and for the professional advice that has helped make this book better than I could have imagined.

I am thankful for you, dear reader. I hope you have enjoyed meeting Phoena and her friends, and that you will return to find out what happens in the next instalment.

Last but not least, thanks to my patient husband Tony, for his constant encouragement, and ongoing support.

Chrissy

A NOTE FROM THE AUTHOR

Greetings from Tasmania, Australia.

Thank you for reading my book.

If you are able, please leave a brief online review, as this will help other readers find my work.

To receive updates about other titles as they are released, please visit www.chrissygarwood.com and complete the form. Links to social media are also listed there.

Publishing a novel was a childhood ambition. In the intervening years, God has brought me through many challenging experiences.

But the adventures my characters endure are works of fiction – a small grain of inspiration, a mountain of imagination, and months of hard work to bring it all together.

I have learned a lot about myself and my ambitions while pursuing the writing dream. The confidence I am gaining as a storyteller is enriched my character. I believe it is making me a humbler disciple of Jesus Christ, a more determined encourager, a better friend.

Chrissy